THE SPRING OF THE YEAR

DA

MW01092195

INTRODUCTION

IT has been my aim in the thirty-nine chapters of the three books in this series to carry my readers through the weeks of all the school year, not however as with a calendar, for that would be more or less wooden and artificial; but by readings, rather, that catch in a large way the spirit of the particular season, that give something definite and specific in the way of suggestions for tramps afield with things to look for and hear and do. Naturally many of the birds and animals and flowers mentioned, as well as woods and aspects of sky and field, are those of my own local environment—of my New England surrounding—and so must differ in some details from those surrounding you in your far Southern home or you on your distant Pacific coast, or you in your rich and varied valley of the Mississippi, or you on your wide and generous prairie. But the similarities and correspondences, the things and conditions we have in common, are more than our differences. Our sun, moon, sky, earth—our land—are the same, our love for this beautiful world is the same, as is that touch of nature which we all feel and which makes us all kin. Wherever, then, in these books of the seasons, the things treated differ from the things around you, read about those things for information, and in your journeys afield fill in the gaps with whatever it is that completes your landscape, or rounds out your cycle of the seasons, or links up your endless chain of life.

While I have tried to be accurate throughout these books, still it has not been my object chiefly to write a natural history—volumes of outdoor facts; but to quicken the imaginations behind the sharp eyes, behind the keen ears and the eager souls of the multitude of children who go to school, as I used to go to school, through an open, stirring, beckoning world of living things that I longed to range and understand.

The best thing that I can do as writer, that you can do as teacher, if I may quote from the last paragraph—the keynote of these volumes—is to "go into the fields and woods, go deep and far and frequently, with eyes and ears and all your souls alert."

MULLEIN HILL, May, 1912

THE SPRING OF THE YEAR

CHAPTER I
"SPRING! SPRING! SPRING!"

WHO is your spring messenger? Is it bird or flower or beast that brings your spring? What sight or sound or smell spells S-P-R-I-N-G to you, in big, joyous letters?

Perhaps it is the frogs. Certainly I could not have a real spring without the frogs. They have peeped "Spring!" to me every time I have had a spring. Perhaps it is the arbutus, or the hepatica, or the pussy-willow, or the bluebird, or the yellow spice-bush, or, if you chance to live in New England, perhaps it is the wood pussy that brings your spring!

Beast, bird, or flower, whatever it is, there comes a day and a messenger and—spring! You know that spring is here. It may snow again before night: no matter; your messenger has brought you the news, brought you the very spring itself, and after all your waiting through the winter months are you going to be discouraged by a flurry of snow?

"All white and still lie stream and hill—
The winter dread and drear!
When from the skies a bluebird flies,
And—spring is here!"

To be sure, it is here, if the bluebird is your herald.

But how much faith in the weather you must have, and how you must long for the spring before the first bluebird brings it to you! Some sunny March day he drops down out of the blue sky, saying softly, sweetly, "Florida, florida!" as if calling the flowers; and then he is gone!—gone for days at a time, while it snows and blows and rains, freezes and thaws, thaws, thaws, until the March mud looks fitter for clams than for flowers.

So it is with the other first signs. If you want springtime ahead of time, then you must have it in your heart, out of reach of the weather, just as you must grow cucumbers in a hothouse if you want them ahead of time. But there comes a day when cucumbers will grow out of doors; and there comes a day when the bluebird and the song sparrow and all the other heralds stay, when spring has come whether you have a heart or not.

What day is that in your out-of-doors, and what sign have you to mark it? Mr. John Burroughs says his sign is the wake-robin, or trillium. When I was a school-boy it used to be for me the arbutus; but nowadays it is the shadbush: I have no sure settled spring until I see the shadbush beginning to open misty white in the edge of the woods. Then I can trust the weather; I can open my beehives; I can plough and plant my garden; I can start into the woods for a day with the birds and flowers; for when the shadbush opens, the great gate to the woods and fields swings open—wide open to let everybody in.

But perhaps you do not know what the shadbush is? That does not matter. You can easily enough find that out. Some call it June-berry; others call it service-berry; and the botany calls it *A-me-lan'chi-er ca-na-den'sis*! But that does not matter either. For this is not a botany lesson. It is an account of how springtime comes to *me*, and when and what are its signs. And I would have you read it to think how springtime comes to *you*, and when and what are its signs. So, if the dandelion, and not the shadbush, is your sign, then you must read "dandelion" here every time I write "shadbush."

There is an old saying, "He that would bring home the wealth of the Indies must carry the wealth of the Indies out"; which is to say, those who bring home the wealth of the Indies, must carry out some kind of wealth in exchange. So you who would enjoy or understand what my shadbush means to me must have a shadbush of your own, or a dandelion, or something that is a sign to you that spring is here. Then, you see, my chapter in the book will become your own.

There are so many persons who do not know one bird from another, one tree from another, one flower from another; who would not know one season from another did they not see the spring hats in the milliner's window or feel the need of a change of coat. I hope you are not one of them. I hope you are on the watch, instead, for the first phœbe or the earliest bloodroot, or are listening to catch the shrill, brave peeping of the little tree-frogs, the hylas.

As for me, I am on the watch for the shadbush. Oh, yes, spring comes before the shadbush opens, but it is likely not to stay. The wild geese trumpet spring in the gray March skies as they pass; a February rain, after a long cold season of snow, spatters your face with spring; the swelling buds on the maples, the fuzzy kittens on the pussy-willows, the opening marsh-marigolds in the meadows, the frogs, the bluebirds—all of these, while they stay, are the spring. But they are not sure to stay over night, here in New England. You may wake up and find it snowing—until the shadbush opens. After that, hang up your sled and skates, put away your overcoat and mittens; for spring is here, and the honey-bees will buzz every bright day until the October asters are in bloom.

I said if you want springtime ahead of time you must have it in your heart. Of course you must. If your heart is warm and your eye is keen, you can go forth in the dead of winter and gather buds, seeds, cocoons, and living things enough to make a little spring. For the fires of summer are never wholly out. They are only banked in the winter, smouldering always under the snow, and quick to brighten and burst into blaze. There comes a warm day in January, and across your thawing path crawls a woolly-bear caterpillar; a mourning-cloak butterfly flits through the woods, and the juncos sing. That night a howling snowstorm sweeps out of the north; the coals are covered again. So they kindle and darken, until they leap from the ashes of winter a pure, thin blaze in the shadbush, to burn higher and hotter across the summer, to flicker and die away—a line of yellow embers—in the weird witch-hazel of the autumn.

At the sign of the shadbush the doors of my springtime swing wide open. My birds are back, my turtles are out, my long sleeping woodchucks are wide awake. There is not a stretch of woodland or meadow now that shows a trace of winter. Over the pasture the bluets are beginning to drift, as if the haze on the distant hills, floating down in the night, had been caught in the dew-wet grass. They wash the field to its borders in their delicate azure hue. At the sign of the shadbush the doors of my memory, too, swing wide open, and I am a boy again in the meadows of my old home. The shadbush is in blossom, and the fish are running—the sturgeon up the Delaware; the shad up Cohansey Creek; and through the Lower Sluice, these soft, stirring nights, the catfish are slipping. Is there any real boy now in Lupton's Meadows to watch them come? Oh yes, doubtless; and doubtless there ever shall be. But I would go down for this one night, down in the May moonlight, and listen, as I used to listen years ago, for the quiet *splash splash splash*, as the swarming catfish pass through the shallows of the main ditch, up toward the dam at the pond.

At the sign of the shadbush how swiftly the tides of life begin to rise! How mysteriously their currents run!—the fish swimming in from the sea, the birds flying up from the South, the flowers opening fresh from the soil, the insects coming out from their sleep: life moving everywhere—across the heavens, over the earth, along the deep, dim aisles of the sea!

CHAPTER II
THE SPRING RUNNING

THIS title is Kipling's; the observations that follow are mine; but the real spring running is yours and mine and Kipling's and Mowgli the wolf-child's, whose running Kipling has told us about. Indeed, every child of the earth has felt it, has had the running—every living thing of the land and the sea.

Everything feels it; everything is restless, everything is moving. The renter changes houses; the city dweller goes "down to the shore" or up to the mountains to open his summer cottage; the farmer starts to break up the land for planting; the schoolchildren begin to squirm in their seats and long to fly out of the windows; and "Where are you *going* this summer?" is on every one's lips.

They have all caught the spring running, the only infection I know that you can catch from April skies. The very sun has caught it, too, and is lengthening out his course, as if he hated to stop and go to bed at night. And the birds, that are supposed to go to bed most promptly, they sleep, says the good old poet Chaucer, with open eye, these April nights, so bad is their case of spring running,—

"So priketh hem Nature in hir corages."[1]

[1] So nature pricks (stirs) them in their hearts.

Their long journey northward over sea and land has not cured them yet of their unrest. Only one thing will do it (and I suppose we all should be glad), one sovereign remedy, and that is *family cares*. But they are yet a long way off.

Meantime watch your turkey-hen, how she saunters down the field alone, how pensive she looks, how lost for something to do and somewhere to go. She is sick with this disease of spring. Follow her, keeping out of sight yourself, and lo, a nest, hidden under a pile of brush in a corner of the pasture fence, half a mile from home!

The turkey-hen has wandered off half a mile to build her nest; but many wild birds have come on their small wings all the way from the forests of the Amazon and have gone on to Hudson Bay and the Fur Countries, just to build their nests and rear their young. A wonderful case of the spring running, you would say; and still more wonderful is the annual journey of the golden plover from Patagonia to Alaska and back, eight thousand miles each way. Yet there is another case that seems to me more mysterious, and quite as wonderful, as the sea seems more mysterious than the land.

It is the spring running of the fish. For when the great tidal waves of bird-life begin to roll northward with the sun, a corresponding movement begins among the denizens of the sea. The cold-blooded fish feel the stirring; the spring running seizes them, and in they come through the pathless wastes of the ocean, waves of them, shoals of them,—sturgeon, shad, herring,—like the waves and flocks of wild geese, warblers, and swallows overhead,—into the brackish water of the bays and rivers and on (the herring) into the fresh water of the ponds.

To watch the herring come up Weymouth Back River into Herring Run here near my home, as I do every April, is to watch one of the most interesting, most mysterious movements of all nature. It was about a century ago that men of Weymouth brought herring in barrels of water by ox-teams from Taunton River and liberated them in the pond at the head of Weymouth Back River. These fish laid their eggs in the grassy margins of the pond that spring and went out down the river to the sea. Later on, the young fry, when large enough to care for themselves, found their way down the river and out to sea.

And where did they go then? and what did they do? Who can tell? for who can read the dark book of the sea? Yet this one thing we know they did, for still they are doing it after all these hundred years,—they came back up the river, when they were full-grown,—up the river, up the run, up into the pond, to lay their eggs in the waters where they were hatched, in the waters that to them were *home*.

Something very much like this all the other fish are doing, as are the birds also. The spell of *home* is over land and sea, and has been laid upon them all. The bird companies of the fall went south at the inexorable command of Hunger; but a greater than Hunger is in command of the forces of spring. Now our vast bird army of North America, five billion strong, is moving northward at the call of Home. And the hosts of the sea, whose shining billions we cannot number,—they, too, are coming up, some of them far up through the shallow streams to the wood-walled ponds for a drink of the sweet waters of Home.

As a boy I used to go down to the meadows at night to hear the catfish coming, as now I go down to the village by day to see the herring coming. The catfish would swim in from the Cohansey, through the sluices in the bank, then up by way of the meadow ditches to the dam over which fall the waters of Lupton's Pond.

It was a seven-or eight-foot dam, and of course the fish could not climb it. Down under the splashing water they would crowd by hundreds, their moving bodies close-packed, pushing forward, all trying to break through the wooden wall that blocked their way. Slow, stupid things they looked; but was not each big cat head pointed forward? each slow, cold brain trying to follow and keep up with each swift, warm heart? For the homeward-bound heart knows no barrier; it never stops for a dam.

The herring, too, on their way up the run are stopped by a dam; but the town, in granting to certain men the sole rights to catch the fish, stipulated that a number of the live herring, as many as several barrels full, should be helped over the dam each spring that they might go on up to the pond to deposit their eggs. If this were not done annually, the fish would soon cease to come, and the Weymouth herring would be no more.

There was no such lift for the catfish under Lupton's dam. I often tossed them over into the pond, and so helped to continue the line; but perhaps there was no need, for spring after spring they returned. They were the young fish, I suppose, new each year, from parent fish that remain inside the pond the year round.

I cannot say now—I never asked myself before—whether it is Mother or Father Catfish who stays with the swarm (it is literally a swarm) of kitten catfish. It may be father, as in the case of Father Stickleback and Father Toadfish, who cares for the children. If it is—I take off my hat to him. I have four of my own; and I think if I had eighteen or twenty more I should have both hands full. But Father Catfish! Did you ever see his brood?

I should say that there might easily be five hundred young ones in the family, though I never have counted them. But you might. If you want to try it, take your small scoop-net of coarse cheesecloth, or mosquito-netting, and go down to the pond this spring. Close along the margin you will see holes in the shallow water running up under the overhanging grass and roots. The holes were made probably by the muskrats. It is in here that the old catfish is guarding the brood.

As soon as you learn to know the holes, you can cover the entrance with your net, and then by jumping or stamping hard on the ground above the hole, you will drive out the old fish with a flop, the family following in a fine, black cloud. The old fish will swim away, then come slowly back to the scattered swarm, to the little black things that look like small tadpoles, who soon cluster about the parent once more and wiggle away into the deep, dark water of the pond—the strangest family group that I know in all the spring world.

CHAPTER III
AN OLD APPLE TREE

BEYOND the meadow, perhaps half a mile from my window, stands an old apple tree, the last of an ancient line that once marked the boundary between the "upper" and the "lower" pastures. It is a bent, broken, hoary old tree, grizzled with suckers from feet to crown. No one has pruned it for half a century; no one ever gathers its gnarly apples—no one but the cattle who love to lie in its shadow and munch its fruit.

The cows know the tree. One of their winding paths runs under its low-hung branches; and as I frequently travel the cow-paths, I also find my way thither. Yet I do not go for apples, nor just because the cow-path takes me. That old apple tree is hollow, hollow all over, trunk and branches, as hollow as a lodging-house; and I have never known it when it was not "putting up" some wayfaring visitor or some permanent lodger. So I go over, whenever I have a chance, to call upon my friends or pay my respects to the distinguished guests.

This old tree is on the neighboring farm. It does not belong to me, and I am glad; for if it did, then I should have to trim it, and scrape it, and plaster up its holes, and put a burlap petticoat on it, all because of the gruesome gypsy moths that infest my trees. Oh, yes, that would make it bear better apples, but what then would become of its birds and beasts? Everybody ought to have *one* apple tree that bears birds and beasts—and Baldwin apples, too, of course, if the three sorts of fruit can be made to grow on the same tree. But only the birds and beasts grow well on the untrimmed, unscraped, unplastered, unpetticoated old tree yonder between the pastures. His heart is wide open to every small traveler passing by.

Whenever I look over toward the old tree, I think of the old vine-covered, weather-beaten house in which my grandfather lived, where many a traveler put up over night—to get a plate of grandmother's buckwheat cakes, I think, and a taste of her keen wit. The old house sat in under a grove of pin oak and pine,—"Underwood" we called it,—a sheltered, sheltering spot; with a peddler's stall in the barn, a peddler's place at the table, a peddler's bed in the herby garret, a boundless, fathomless featherbed, of a piece with the house and the hospitality. There were larger houses and newer, in the neighborhood; but no other house in all the region, not even the tavern, two miles farther down the pike, was half so central, or so homelike, or so full of sweet and juicy gossip. The old apple tree yonder between the woods and the meadow is as central, as hospitable, and, if animals talk with one another, just as full of neighborhood news as was grandfather's roof-tree.

Of course you would never suspect it, passing by. But then, no lover of wild things passes by—never without first stopping, and especially before an old tree all full of holes. Whenever you see a hole in a tree, in a sand-bank, in a hillside, under a rail-pile—anywhere out of doors, stop!

Stop here beside this decrepit apple tree. No, you will find no sign swinging from the front, no door-plate, no letter-box bearing the name of the family residing here. The birds and beasts do not advertise their houses so. They would hide their houses, they would have you pass by; for most persons are rude in the woods and fields, breaking into the homes of the wood-folk as they never would dream of doing in the case of their human neighbors.

There is no need of being rude anywhere, no need of being an unwelcome visitor even to the shyest and most timid of the little people of the fields. Come over with me—they know me in the old apple tree. It is nearly sundown. The evening is near, with night at its heels, for it is an early March day.

We shall not wait long. The doors will open that we may enter—enter into a home of the fields, and, a little way at least, into a life of the fields, for, as I have said, this old tree has a small dweller of some sort the year round.

On this March day we shall be admitted by my owls. They take possession late in winter and occupy the tree, with some curious fellow tenants, until early summer. I can count upon these small screech owls by February,—the forlorn month, the seasonless, hopeless, lifeless month of the year, but for its owls, its thaws, its lengthening days, its cackling pullets, its possible bluebirds, and its being the year's end! At least the ancients called February, not December, the year's end, maintaining, with some sense, that the making of the world was begun in March, that is, with the spring. The owls do not, like the swallows, bring the spring, but they nevertheless help winter with most seemly haste into an early grave.

If, as the dusk comes down, I cannot go over to the tree, I will go to my window and watch. I cannot see him, the grim-beaked baron with his hooked talons, his ghostly wings, his night-seeing eyes, but I know that he has come to his window in the apple-tree turret yonder against the darkening sky, and that he watches with me. I cannot see him swoop downward over the ditches, nor see him quarter the meadow, beating, dangling, dropping between the flattened tussocks; nor can I hear him, as, back on the silent shadows, he slants upward again to his tower. Mine are human eyes, human ears. Even the quick-eared meadow mouse did not hear until the long talons closed and it was too late.

SCREECH OWL—"OUT OVER THE MEADOW HE SAILS"

But there have been times when, like some belated traveler, I have been forced to cross this wild night-land of his; and I have *felt* him pass—so near at times that he has stirred my hair, by the wind—dare I say?—of his mysterious wings. At other times I have heard him. Often on the edge of night I have listened to his quavering, querulous cry from the elm-tops below me by the meadow. But oftener I have watched at the casement here in my castle wall.

Away yonder on the borders of night, dim and gloomy, looms his ancient keep. I wait. Soon on the deepened dusk spread his soft wings, out over the meadow he sails, up over my wooded height, over my moat, to my turret tall, as silent and unseen as the soul of a shadow, except he drift across the face of the full round moon, or with his weird cry cause the dreaming quiet to stir in its sleep and moan.

Now let us go over again to the old tree, this time in May. It will be curious enough, as the soft dusk comes on, to see the round face of the owl in one hole and, out of another hole in the broken limb above, the flat, weazened face of a little tree-toad.

Both creatures love the dusk; both have come forth to their open doors to watch the darkening; both will make off under the cover of the night—one for mice and frogs over the meadow, the other for slugs and insects over the crooked, tangled limbs of the apple tree.

It is strange enough to see them together, but it is stranger still to think of them together; for it is just such prey as this little toad that the owl has gone over the meadow to catch.

Why does he not take the supper ready here on the shelf? There may be reasons that we, who do not eat tree-toad, know nothing of; but I am inclined to believe that the owl has never seen his fellow lodger in the doorway above, though he must often have heard him trilling gently and lonesomely in the gloaming, when his skin cries for rain!

Small wonder if they have never met! for this gray, squat, disk-toed little monster in the hole, or flattened on the bark of the tree like a patch of lichen, may well be one of the things that are hidden from even the sharp-eyed owl. It is always a source of fresh amazement, the way that this largest of the hylas, on the moss-marked rind of an old tree, can utterly blot himself out before your staring eyes.

The common toads and all the frogs have enemies enough, and it would seem from the comparative scarcity of the tree-toads that they must have enemies, too; but I do not know who

5

they are. This scarcity of the tree-toads is something of a puzzle, and all the more to me, that, to my certain knowledge, this toad has lived in the old Baldwin tree, now, for five years. Perhaps he has been several toads, you say, not one; for who can tell one tree-toad from another? Nobody; and for that reason I made, some time ago, a simple experiment, in order to see how long a tree-toad might live, unprotected, in his own natural environment.

Upon moving into this house, about nine years ago, we found a tree-toad living in the big hickory by the porch. For the next three springs he reappeared, and all summer long we would find him, now on the tree, now on the porch, often on the railing and backed tight up against a post. Was he one or many? we asked. Then we marked him; and for the next four years we knew that he was himself alone. How many more years he might have lived in the hickory for us all to pet, I should like to know; but last summer, to our great sorrow, the gypsy moth killers, poking in the hole, hit our little friend and left him dead.

It was very wonderful to me, the instinct for home—the love for home, I should like to call it—that this humble little creature showed. Now, a toad is an amphibian to the zoölogist; an ugly gnome with a jeweled eye, to the poet; but to the naturalist, the lover of life for its own sake, who lives next door to his toad, who feeds him a fly or a fat grub now and then, who tickles him to sleep with a rose leaf, who waits as thirstily as the hilltop for him to call the summer rain, who knows his going to sleep for the winter, his waking up for the spring—to such a one, I say, a tree-toad means more than the jeweled eye and the strange amphibious habits.

This small tree-toad had a home, had it in a tree, too,—in a hickory tree,—this toad that dwelt by my house.

"East, west,
Hame's best,"

croaked our tree-toad in a tremulous, plaintive song that wakened memories in the vague twilight of more old, unhappy, far-off things than any other voice I ever knew.

These two tree-toads could not have been induced to trade houses, the hickory for the apple, because a house to a toad means home, and a home is never in the market. There are many more houses in the land than homes. Most of us are only real-estate dealers. Many of us have never had a home; and none of us has ever had, perhaps, more than one, or could have—that home of our childhood.

This toad seemed to feel it all. Here in the hickory for four years (more nearly seven, I am sure) he lived, single and alone. He would go down to the meadow when the toads gathered there to lay their eggs; but back he would come, without mate or companion, to his tree. Stronger than love of kind, than love of mate, constant and dominant in his slow cold heart was his instinct for home.

If I go down to the orchard and bring up from an apple tree some other toad to dwell in the hole of the hickory, I shall fail. He might remain for the day, but not throughout the night, for with the gathering twilight there steals upon him an irresistible longing; and guided by it, as bee and pigeon and dog and man are guided, he makes his sure way back to his orchard home.

Would my toad of the Baldwin tree go back beyond the orchard, over the road, over the wide meadow, over to the old tree, half a mile away, if I brought him from there? We shall see. During the coming summer I shall mark him in some manner, and bringing him here to the hickory, I shall then watch the old apple tree yonder to see if he returns. It will be a hard, perilous journey. But his longing will not let him rest; and, guided by his mysterious sense of direction,—for that *one* place,—he will arrive, I am sure, or he will die on the way.

Suppose he never gets back? Only one toad less? A great deal more than that. There in the old Baldwin he has made his home for I don't know how long, hunting over its world of branches in the summer, sleeping down in its deep holes during the winter—down under the chips and punk and castings, beneath the nest of the owls, it may be; for my toad in the hickory always buried himself so, down in the débris at the bottom of the hole, where, in a kind of cold storage, he preserved himself until thawed out by the spring.

I never pass the old apple in the summer but that I stop to pay my respects to the toad; nor in the winter that I do not pause and think of him asleep in there. He is no longer mere toad. He has passed into the Guardian Spirit of the tree, warring in the green leaf against worm and grub and slug, and in the dry leaf hiding himself, a heart of life, within the thin ribs, as if to save the old shell of a tree to another summer.

Often in the dusk, especially the summer dusk, I have gone over to sit at his feet and learn some of the things that my school-teachers and college professors did not teach me.

Seating myself comfortably at the foot of the tree, I wait. The toad comes forth to the edge of his hole above me, settles himself comfortably, and waits. And the lesson begins. The quiet of the summer evening steals out with the wood-shadows and softly covers the fields. We do not stir. An hour passes. We do not stir. Not to stir is the lesson—one of the primary lessons in this course with the toad.

The dusk thickens. The grasshoppers begin to strum; the owl slips out and drifts away; a whip-poor-will drops on the bare knoll near me, clucks and shouts and shouts again, his rapid repetition a thousand times repeated by the voices that call to one another down the long empty aisles of the swamp; a big moth whirs about my head and is gone; a bat flits squeaking past; a firefly blazes, is blotted out by the darkness, blazes again, and so passes, his tiny lantern flashing into a night that seems the darker for his quick, unsteady glow.

We do not stir. It is a hard lesson. By all my other teachers I had been taught every manner of stirring, and this strange exercise of being still takes me where my body is weakest, and puts me almost out of breath.

What! out of breath by keeping still? Yes, because I had been hurrying hither and thither, doing this and that—doing them so fast for so many years that I no longer understood how to sit down and keep still and do nothing inside of me as well as outside. Of course *you* know how to keep still, for you are children. And so perhaps you do not need to take lessons of teacher Toad. But I do, for I am grown up, and a man, with a world of things to do, a great many of which I do not need to do at all—if only I would let the toad teach me all he knows.

So, when I am tired, I will go over to the toad. I will sit at his feet, where time is nothing, and the worry of work even less. He has all time and no task. He sits out the hour silent, thinking—I know not what, nor need to know. So we will sit in silence, the toad and I, watching Altair burn along the shore of the horizon, and overhead Arcturus, and the rival fireflies flickering through the leaves of the apple tree. And as we watch, I shall have time to rest and to think. Perhaps I shall have a thought, a thought all my own, a rare thing for any one to have, and worth many an hour of waiting.

CHAPTER IV
A CHAPTER OF THINGS TO SEE THIS SPRING

OUT of the multitude of sights, which twelve sights this spring shall I urge you to see? Why the twelve, of course, that I always look for most eagerly. And the first of these, I think, is the bluebird.

I

"Have you seen a bluebird yet?" some friend will ask me, as March comes on. Or it will be, "I have seen my first bluebird!" as if seeing a first bluebird were something very wonderful and important. And so it is; for the sight of the first March bluebird is the last sight of winter and the first sight of spring. The brown of the fertile earth is on its breast, the blue of the summer sky is on its back, and in its voice is the clearest, sweetest of all invitations to come out of doors.

Where has he spent the winter? Look it up. What has brought him back so early? Guess at it. What does he say as he calls to you? Listen. What has John Burroughs written about him? Look it up and read.

II

You must see the skunk-cabbage abloom in the swamp. You need not pick it and carry it home for the table—just see it. But be sure you see it. Get down and open the big purple-streaked spathe, as it spears the cold mud, and look at the "spadix" covered with its tiny but perfect flowers. Now wait a minute. The woods are still bare; ice may still be found on the northern slopes, while here before you, like a wedge splitting the frozen soil, like a spear cleaving through the earth from the other, the summer, side of the world, is this broad blade of life letting up almost the first cluster of the new spring's flowers. Wait a moment longer and you may hear your first bumblebee, as he comes humming at the door of the cabbage for a taste of new honey and pollen.

III

Among the other early signs of spring, you should see a flock of red-winged blackbirds! And what a sight they are upon a snow-covered field! For often after their return it will snow again, when the brilliant, shining birds in black with their red epaulets make one of the most striking sights of the season.

IV

Another bird event that you should witness is the arrival of the migrating warblers. You will be out one of these early May days when there will be a stirring of small birds in the bushes at your side, in the tall trees over your head—everywhere! It is the warblers. You are in the tide of the tiny migrants—yellow warblers, pine warblers, myrtle warblers, black-throated green warblers—some of them on their way from South America to Labrador. You must be in the woods and see them as they come.

V

You should see the "spice-bush" (wild allspice or fever-bush or Benjamin-bush) in bloom in the damp March woods. And, besides that, you should see with your own eyes under some deep, dark forest trees the blue hepatica and on some bushy hillside the pink arbutus. (For fear I forget to tell you in the chapter of things to do, let me now say that you should take a day this spring and go "may-flowering.")

VI

There are four nests that you should see this spring: a hummingbird's nest, saddled upon the horizontal limb of some fruit or forest tree, and looking more like a wart on the limb than a nest; secondly, the nest, eggs rather, of a turtle buried in the soft sand along the margin of a pond or out in some cultivated field; thirdly, the nest of a sun-fish (pumpkin-seed) in the shallow water close up along the sandy shore of the pond; and fourthly, the nest of the red squirrel, made of fine stripped cedar bark, away up in the top of some tall pine tree! I mean by this that there are many other interesting nest-builders besides the birds. Of all the difficult nests to find, the hummingbird's is the most difficult. When you find one, please write to me about it.

VII

You should see a "spring peeper," the tiny Pickering's frog—*if you can*. The marsh and the meadows will be vocal with them, but one of the hardest things that you will try to do this spring will be to see the shrill little piper, as he plays his bagpipe in the rushes at your very feet. But hunt until you do see him. It will sharpen your eyes and steady your patience for finding other things.

VIII

You should see the sun come up on a May morning. The dawn is always a wonderful sight, but never at other times attended with quite the glory, with quite the music, with quite the sweet fragrance, with quite the wonder of a morning in May. Don't fail to see it. Don't fail to rise with it. You will feel as if you had wings—something better even than wings.

IX

You should see a farmer ploughing in a large field—the long straight furrows of brown earth; the blackbirds following behind after worms; the rip of the ploughshare; the roll of the soil from the smooth mould-board—the wealth of it all. For in just such fields is the wealth of the world, and the health of it, too. Don't miss the sight of the ploughing.

X

Go again to the field, three weeks later, and see it all green with sprouting corn, or oats, or one of a score of crops. Then—but in "The Fall of the Year" I ask you to go once more and see that field all covered with shocks of ripened corn, shocks that are pitched up and down its long rows of corn-butts like a vast village of Indian tepees, each tepee full of golden corn.

XI

You should see, hanging from a hole in some old apple tree, a long thin snake-skin! It is the latch-string of the great crested flycatcher. Now why does this bird always use a snake-skin in his nest? and why does he usually leave it hanging loose outside the hole? Questions, these, for you to think about. And if you will look sharp, you will see in even the commonest things questions enough to keep you thinking as long as you live.

XII

You should see a dandelion. A dandelion? Yes, a dandelion, "fringing the dusty road with harmless gold." But that almost requires four eyes—two to see the dandelion and two more to see the gold—the two eyes in your head, and the two in your imagination. Do you really know how to see anything? Most persons have eyes, but only a few really see. This is because they cannot look hard and steadily at anything. The first great help to real seeing is to go into the woods knowing what you hope to see—seeing it in your eye, as we say, before you see it in the out-of-doors. No one would ever see a tree-toad on a mossy tree or a whip-poor-will among the fallen leaves who did not have tree-toads and whip-poor-wills in mind. Then, secondly, look at the thing *hard* until you see in it something peculiar, something different from anything like it that you ever saw before. Don't dream in the woods; don't expect the flowers to tell you their names or the wild things to come up and ask you to wait while they perform for you.

CHAPTER V
IF YOU HAD WINGS

IF you had wings, why of course you would wear feathers instead of clothes, and you might be a crow! And then of course you would steal corn, and run the risk of getting three of your big wing feathers shot away.

8

All winter long, and occasionally during this spring, I have seen one of my little band of crows flying about with a big hole in his wing,—at least three of his large wing feathers gone, shot away probably last summer,—which causes him to fly with a list or limp, like an automobile with a flattened tire, or a ship with a shifted ballast.

Now for nearly a year that crow has been hobbling about on one whole and one half wing, trusting to luck to escape his enemies, until he can get three new feathers to take the places of those that are missing. "Well, why doesn't he get them?" you ask. If you were that crow, how would you get them? Can a crow, by taking thought, add three new feathers to his wing?

Certainly not. That crow must wait until wing-feather season comes again, just as an apple tree must wait until apple-growing season comes to hang its boughs with luscious fruit. The crow has nothing to do with it. His wing feathers are supplied by Nature once a year (after the nesting-time), and if a crow loses any of them, even if right after the new feathers had been supplied, that crow will have to wait until the season for wing feathers comes around once more—if indeed he can wait and does not fall a prey to hawk or owl or the heavy odds of winter.

But Nature is not going to be hurried on that account, nor caused to change one jot or tittle from her wise and methodical course. The Bible says that the hairs of our heads are numbered. So are the feathers on a crow's body. Nature knows just how many there are altogether; how many there are of each sort—primaries, secondaries, tertials, greater coverts, middle coverts, lesser coverts, and scapulars—in the wing; just how each sort is arranged; just when each sort is to be moulted and renewed. If Master Crow does not take care of hisclothes, then he will have to go without until the time for a new suit comes; for Mother Nature won't patch them up as your mother patches up yours.

But now this is what I want you to notice and think about: that just as an apple falls according to a great law of Nature, so a bird's feathers fall according to a law of Nature. The moon is appointed for seasons; the sun knoweth his going down; and so light and insignificant a thing as a bird's feather not only is appointed to grow in a certain place at a certain time, but also knoweth its falling off.

Nothing could look more haphazard, certainly, than the way a hen's feathers seem to drop off at moulting time. The most forlorn, undone, abject creature about the farm is the half-moulted hen. There is one in the chicken-yard now, so nearly naked that she really is ashamed of herself, and so miserably helpless that she squats in a corner all night, unable to reach the low poles of the roost. It is a critical experience with the hen, this moulting of her feathers; and were it not for the protection of the yard it would be a fatal experience, so easily could she be captured. Nature seems to have no hand in the business at all; if she has, then what a mess she is making of it!

But pick up the hen, study the falling of the feathers carefully, and lo! here is law and order, every feather as important to Nature as a star, every quill as a planet, and the old white hen as mightily looked after by Nature as the round sphere of the universe!

Once a year, usually after the nesting-season, it seems a physical necessity for most birds to renew their plumage.

We get a new suit (some of us) because our old one wears out. That is the most apparent cause for the new annual suit of the birds. Yet with them, as with some of us, the feathers go out of fashion, and then the change of feathers is a mere matter of style, it seems.

For severe and methodical as Mother Nature must be (and what mother or teacher or ruler, who has great things to do and a multitude of little things to attend to, must not be severe and methodical?)—severe, I say, as Mother Nature must be in looking after her children's clothes, she has for all that a real motherly heart, it seems.

For see how she looks after their wedding garments—giving to most of the birds a new suit, gay and gorgeous, especially to the bridegrooms, as if fine feathers *did* make a fine bird! Or does she do all of this to meet the fancy of the bride, as the scientists tell us? Whether so or not, it is a fact that among the birds it is the bridegroom who is adorned for his wife, and sometimes the fine feathers come by a special moult—an extra suit for him!

Take Bobolink, for instance. He has two complete moults a year, two new suits, one of them his wedding suit. Now, as I write, I hear him singing over the meadow—a jet-black, white, and cream-buff lover, most strikingly adorned. His wife, down in the grass, looks as little like him as a sparrow looks like a blackbird. But after the breeding-season he will moult again, changing color so completely that he and his wife and children will all look alike, all like sparrows, and will even lose their names, flying south now under the name of "reed-birds."

Bobolink passes the winter in Brazil; and in the spring, just before the long northward journey begins, he lays aside his fall traveling clothes and puts on his gay wedding garments and starts north for his bride. But you would hardly know he was so dressed, to look at him; for, strangely enough, he is not black and white, but still colored like a sparrow, as he was in the

9

fall. *Apparently* he is. Look at him more closely, however, and you will find that the brownish-yellow color is all caused by a veil of fine fringes hanging from the edges of the feathers. The bridegroom wearing the wedding veil? Yes! Underneath is the black and white and cream-buff suit. He starts northward; and, by the time he reaches Massachusetts, the fringe veil is worn off and the black and white bobolink appears. Specimens taken after their arrival here still show traces of the brownish-yellow veil.

Many birds do not have this early spring moult at all; and with most of those that do, the great wing feathers are not then renewed as are bobolink's, but only at the annual moult after the nesting is done. The great feathers of the wings are, as you know, the most important feathers a bird has; and the shedding of them is so serious a matter that Nature has come to make the change according to the habits and needs of the birds. With most birds the body feathers begin to go first, then the wing feathers, and last those of the tail. But the shedding of the wing feathers is a very slow and carefully regulated process.

In the wild geese and other water birds the wing feathers drop out with the feathers of the body, and go so nearly together that the birds really cannot fly. On land you could catch the birds with your hands. But they keep near or on the water and thus escape, though times have been when it was necessary to protect them at this season by special laws; for bands of men would go into their nesting-marshes and kill them with clubs by hundreds!

The shedding of the feathers brings many risks to the birds; but Nature leaves none of her children utterly helpless. The geese at this time cannot fly because their feathers are gone; but they can swim, and so get away from most of their natural enemies. On the other hand, the hawks that hunt by wing, and must have wings always in good feather, or else perish, lose their feathers so slowly that they never feel their loss. It takes a hawk nearly a year to get a complete change of wing feathers, one or two dropping out from each wing at a time, at long intervals apart.

Then here is the gosling, that goes six weeks in down, before it gets its first feathers, which it sheds within a few weeks, in the fall. Whereas the young quail is born with quills so far grown that it is able to fly almost as soon as it is hatched. These are real mature feathers; but the bird is young and soon outgrows these first flight feathers, so they are quickly lost and new ones come. This goes on till fall, *several* moults occurring the first summer to meet the increasing weight of the little quail's growing body.

I said that Nature was severe and methodical, and so she is, where she needs to be, so severe that you are glad, perhaps, that you are not a crow. But Nature, like every wise mother, is severe only where she needs to be. A crow's wing feathers are vastly important to him. Let him then take care of them, for they are the best feathers made and are put in to stay a year. But a crow's tail feathers are not so vastly important to him; he could get on, if, like the rabbit in the old song, he had no tail at all.

In most birds the tail is a kind of balance or steering-gear, and not of equal importance with the wings. Nature, consequently, seems to have attached less importance to the feathers of the tail. They are not so firmly set, nor are they of the same quality or kind; for, unlike the wing feathers, if a tail feather is lost through accident, it is made good, no matter when. How do you explain it? Do you think I believe that old story of the birds roosting with their tails out, so that, because of generations of lost tails, those feathers now grow expecting to be plucked by some enemy, and therefore have only a temporary hold?

The normal, natural way, of course, is to replace a lost feather with a new one as soon as possible. But, in order to give extra strength to the wing feathers, Nature has found it necessary to check their frequent change; and so complete is the check that the annual moult is required to replace a single one. The Japanese have discovered the secret of this check, and are able by it to keep certain feathers in the tails of their cocks growing until they reach the enormous length of ten to twelve feet.

My crow, it seems, lost his three feathers last summer just after his annual moult; the three broken shafts he carries still in his wing, and must continue to carry, as the stars must continue their courses, until those three feathers have rounded out their cycle to the annual moult. The universe of stars and feathers is a universe of law, of order, and of reason.

CHAPTER VI
A CHAPTER OF THINGS TO DO THIS SPRING

I DO not know where to begin—there are so many interesting things to do this spring! But, while we ought to be interested in all of the out-of-doors, it is very necessary to select some *one* field, say, the birds or flowers, for *special* study. That would help us to decide what to do this spring.

I

If there is still room under your window, or on the clothes-pole in your yard, or in a neighboring tree, nail up another bird-house. (Get "Methods of Attracting Birds" by Gilbert H. Trafton.) If the bird-house is on a pole or post, invert a large tin pan over the end of the post and nail the house fast upon it. This will keep cats and squirrels from disturbing the birds. If the bird-house is in a tree, saw off a limb, if you can without hurting the tree, and do the same there. Cats are our birds' worst enemies.

II

Cats! Begin in your own home and neighborhood a campaign against the cats, to reduce their number and to educate their owners to the need of keeping them well fed and shut up in the house from early evening until after the early morning; for these are the cats' natural hunting hours, when they do the greatest harm to the birds.

This does not mean any cruelty to the cat—no stoning, no persecution. The cat is not at fault. It is the keepers of the cats who need to be educated. Out of every hundred nests in my neighborhood the cats of two farmhouses destroy ninety-five! The state must come to the rescue of the birds by some new rigid law reducing the number of cats.

III

Speaking of birds, let me urge you to begin your watching and study early—with the first robins and bluebirds—and to select some near-by park or wood-lot or meadow to which you can go frequently. There is a good deal in getting intimately acquainted with a locality, so that you know its trees individually, its rocks, walls, fences, the very qualities of its soil. Therefore you want a small area, close at hand. Most observers make the mistake of roaming first here, then there, spending their time and observation in finding their way around, instead of upon the birds to be seen. You must get used to your paths and trees before you can see the birds that flit about them.

IV

In this haunt that you select for your observation, you must study not only the birds but the trees, and the other forms of life, and the shape of the ground (the "lay" of the land) as well, so as to know *all* that you see. In a letter just received from a teacher, who is also a college graduate, occurs this strange description: "My window faces a hill on which straggle brown houses among the deep green of elms or oaks or maples, I don't know which." Perhaps the hill is far away; but I suspect that the writer, knowing my love for the out-of-doors, wanted to give me a vivid picture, but, not knowing one tree from another, put them all in so I could make my own choice!

Learn your common trees, common flowers, common bushes, common animals, along with the birds.

V

Plant a garden, if only a pot of portulacas, and *care* for it, and watch it grow! Learn to dig in the soil and to love it. It is amazing how much and how many things you can grow in a box on the window-sill, or in a corner of the dooryard. There are plants for the sun and plants for the shade, plants for the wall, plants for the very cellar of your house. Get you a bit of earth and plant it, no matter how busy you are with other things this spring.

VI

There are four excursions that you should make this spring: one to a small pond in the woods; one to a deep, wild swamp; one to a wide salt marsh or fresh-water meadow; and one to the seashore—to a wild rocky or sandy shore uninhabited by man.

There are particular birds and animals as well as plants and flowers that dwell only in these haunts; besides, you will get a sight of four distinct kinds of landscape, four deep impressions of the face of nature that are altogether as good to have as the sight of four flowers or birds.

VII

Make a calendar of *your* spring (read "Nature's Diary" by Francis H. Allen)—when and where you find your first bluebird, robin, oriole, etc.; when and where you find your first hepatica, arbutus, saxifrage, etc.; and, as the season goes on, when and where the doings of the various wild things take place.

VIII

Boy or girl, you should go fishing—down to the pond or the river where you go to watch the birds. Suppose you do not catch any fish. That doesn't matter; for you have gone out to the pond with a pole in your hands (a pole is a *real* thing); you have gone with the *hope* (hope is a *real* thing) of catching *fish* (fish are *real* things); and even if you catch no fish, you will be sure, as you wait for the fish to bite, to hear a belted kingfisher, or see a painted turtle, or catch the breath of the sweet leaf-buds and clustered catkins opening around the wooded pond. It is a very good thing for the young naturalist to learn to sit still. A fish-pole is a great help in learning that necessary lesson.

IX

One of the most interesting things you can do for special study is to collect some frogs' eggs from the pond and watch them grow into tadpoles and on into frogs. There are glass vessels made particularly for such study (an ordinary glass jar will do). If you can afford a small glass aquarium, get one and with a few green water plants put in a few minnows, a snail or two, a young turtle, water-beetles, and frogs' eggs, and watch them grow.

X

You should get up by half past three o'clock (at the earliest streak of dawn) and go out into the new morning with the birds! You will hardly recognize the world as that in which your humdrum days (there are no such days, really) are spent! All is fresh, all is new, and the bird-chorus! "Is it possible," you will exclaim, "that this can be the earth?"

Early morning and toward sunset are the best times of the day for bird-study. But if there was not a bird, there would be the sunrise and the sunset—the wonder of the waking, the peace of the closing, day.

XI

I am not going to tell you that you should make a collection of beetles or butterflies (you should *not* make a collection of birds or birds' eggs) or of pressed flowers or of minerals or of arrow-heads or of—anything. Because, while such a collection is of great interest and of real value in teaching you names and things, still there are better ways of studying living nature. For instance, I had rather have you tame a hop-toad, feed him, watch him evening after evening all summer, than make any sort of dead or dried or pressed collection of anything. Live things are better than those things dead. Better know one live toad under your doorstep than bottle up in alcohol all the reptiles of your state.

XII

Finally you should remember that kindliness and patience and close watching are the keys to the out-of-doors; that only sympathy and gentleness and quiet are welcome in the fields and woods. What, then, ought I to say that you should do finally?

CHAPTER VII
THE PALACE IN THE PIG-PEN

"YOU have taken a handful of my wooded acres," says Nature to me, "and if you have not improved them, you at least have changed them greatly. But they are mine still. Be friendly now, go softly, and you shall have them all—and I shall have them all, too. We will share them together."

And we do. Every part of the fourteen acres is mine, yielding some kind of food or fuel or shelter. And every foot, yes, every foot, is Nature's; as entirely hers as when the thick primeval forest stood here. The apple trees are hers as much as mine, and she has ten different bird families that I know of, living in them this spring. A pair of crows and a pair of red-tailed hawks are nesting in the wood-lot; there are at least three families of chipmunks in as many of my stone-piles; a fine old tree-toad sleeps on the porch under the climbing rose; a hornet's nest hangs in a corner of the eaves; a small colony of swifts thunder in the chimney; swallows twitter in the hay-loft; a chipmunk and a half-tame gray squirrel feed in the barn; and—to bring an end to this bare beginning—under the roof of the pig-pen dwell a pair of phœbes.

To make a bird-house of a pig-pen, to divide it between the pig and the bird—this is as far as Nature can go, and this is certainly enough to redeem the whole farm. For she has not sent an outcast or a scavenger to dwell in the pen, but a bird of character, however much he may lack in song or color. Phœbe does not make up well in a picture; neither does he perform well as a singer; there is little to him, in fact, but personality—personality of a kind and (may I say?) quantity, sufficient to make the pig-pen a decent and respectable neighborhood.

Phœbe is altogether more than his surroundings. Every time I go to feed the pig, he lights upon a post near by and says to me, "It's what you are! Not what you do, but how you do it!"—with a launch into the air, a whirl, an unerring snap at a cabbage butterfly, and an easy drop to the post again, by way of illustration. "Not where you live, but how you live there; not the feathers you wear, but how you wear them—it is what you are that counts!"

There is a difference between being a "character" and having one. My phœbe "lives over the pig," but I cannot feel familiar with a bird of his air and carriage, who faces the world so squarely, who settles upon a stake as if he owned it, who lives a prince in my pig-pen.

Look at him! How alert, able, free! Notice the limber drop of his tail, the ready energy it suggests. By that one sign you would know the bird had force. He is afraid of nothing, not even the cold; and he migrates only because he is a flycatcher, and is thus compelled to. The earliest spring day, however, that you find the flies buzzing in the sun, look for phœbe. He is back, coming alone and long before it is safe. He was one of the first of my birds to return this spring.

And it was a fearful spring, this of which I am telling you. How Phœbe managed to exist those miserable March days is a mystery. He came directly to the pen as he had come the year before, and his presence in that bleakest of Marches gave the weather its only touch of spring.

The same force and promptness are manifest in the domestic affairs of the bird. One of the first to arrive this spring, he was the first to build and bring off a brood—or, perhaps, *she* was. And the size of the brood—of the broods, for there was a second, and a third!

Phœbe appeared without his mate, and for nearly three weeks he hunted in the vicinity of the pen, calling the day long, and, toward the end of the second week, occasionally soaring into the air, fluttering, and pouring forth a small, ecstatic song that seemed fairly forced from him.

These aerial bursts meant just one thing: *she* was coming, was coming soon! Was she coming or was he getting ready to go for her? Here he had been for nearly three weeks, his house-lot chosen, his mind at rest, his heart beating faster with every sunrise. It was as plain as day that he knew—was certain—just how and just when something lovely was going to happen. I wished I knew. I was half in love with her myself; and I, too, watched for her.

On the evening of April 14th, he was alone as usual. The next morning a pair of phœbes flitted in and out of the windows of the pen. Here she was. Will some one tell me all about it? Had she just come along and fallen instantly in love with him and his fine pig-pen? It is pretty evident that he nested here last year. Was she, then, his old mate? Did they keep together all through the autumn and winter? If so, then why not together all the way back from Florida to Massachusetts?

Here is a pretty story. But who will tell it to me?

For several days after she came, the weather continued raw and wet, so that nest-building was greatly delayed. The scar of an old, last year's nest still showed on a stringer, and I wondered if they had decided on this or some other site for the new nest. They had not made up their minds, for when they did start it was to make three beginnings in as many places.

Then I offered a suggestion. Out of a bit of stick, branching at right angles, I made a little bracket and tacked it up on one of the stringers. It appealed to them at once, and from that moment the building went steadily on.

Saddled upon this bracket, and well mortared to the stringer, the nest, when finished, was as safe as a castle. And how perfect a thing it was! Few nests, indeed, combine the solidity, the softness, and the exquisite inside curve of Phœbe's.

In placing the bracket, I had carelessly nailed it under one of the cracks in the loose board roof. The nest was receiving its first linings when there came a long, hard rain that beat through the crack and soaked the little cradle. This was serious, for a great deal of mud had been worked into the thick foundation, and here, in the constant shade, the dampness would be long in drying out.

The builders saw the mistake, too, and with their great good sense immediately began to remedy it. They built the bottom up thicker, carried the walls over on a slant that brought the outermost point within the line of the crack, then raised them until the cup was as round-rimmed and hollow as the mould of Mrs. Phœbe's breast could make it.

The outside of the nest, its base, is broad and rough and shapeless enough; but nothing could be softer and lovelier than the inside, the cradle, and nothing drier, for the slanting walls of the nest shed every drop from the leafy crack above.

Wet weather followed the heavy rain until long after the nest was finished. The whole structure was as damp and cold as a newly plastered house. It felt wet to my touch. Yet I noticed that the birds were already brooding. Every night and often during the day I would see one of them in the nest—so deep in, that only a head or a tail showed over the round rim.

After several days I looked to see the eggs, but to my surprise found the nest empty. It had been robbed, I thought, yet by what creature I could not imagine. Then down cuddled one of the birds again—and I understood. Instead of wet and cold, the nest to-day was warm to my hand, and dry almost to the bottom. It had changed color, too, all the upper part having turned a soft silver-gray. She (I am sure it was she) had not been brooding her eggs at all; she had been brooding her mother's thought of them; and for them had been nestling here these days and nights, *drying and warming* their damp cradle with the fire of her life and love.

In due time the eggs came,—five of them, white, spotless, and shapely. While the little phœbe hen was hatching them, I gave my attention further to the cock.

Our intimate friendship revealed a most pleasing nature in phœbe. Perhaps such close and continued association would show like qualities in every bird, even in the kingbird; but I fear only a woman, like Mrs. Olive Thorne Miller, could find them in him. Not much can be said of this flycatcher family, except that it is useful—a kind of virtue that gets its chief reward in heaven. I am acquainted with only four of the other nine Eastern members,—crested flycatcher, kingbird, wood pewee, and chebec,—and each of these has some redeeming attribute besides the habit of catching flies.

They are all good nest-builders, good parents, and brave, independent birds; but aside from phœbe and pewee—the latter in his small way the sweetest voice of the oak woods—the whole family is an odd lot, cross-grained, cross-looking, and about as musical as a family of ducks. A duck seems to know that he cannot sing. A flycatcher knows nothing of his shortcomings. He believes he can sing, and in time he will prove it. If desire and effort count for anything, he certainly must prove it in time. How long the family has already been training, no one knows. Everybody knows, however, the success each flycatcher of them has thus far attained. It would make a good minstrel show, doubtless, if the family would appear together. In chorus, surely, they would be far from a tuneful choir. Yet individually, in the wide universal chorus of the out-of-doors, how much we should miss the kingbird's metallic twitter and the chebec's insistent call!

There was little excitement for phœbe during this period of incubation. He hunted in the neighborhood and occasionally called to his mate, contented enough perhaps, but certainly sometimes appearing tired.

PHŒBE AND HER YOUNG

One rainy day he sat in the pig-pen window looking out at the gray, wet world. He was humped and silent and meditative, his whole attitude speaking the extreme length of his day, the monotony of the drip, drip, drip from the eaves, and the sitting, the ceaseless sitting, of his brooding wife. He might have hastened the time by catching a few flies for her or by taking her place on the nest; but I never saw him do it.

Things were livelier when the eggs hatched, for it required a good many flies a day to keep the five young ones growing. And how they grew! Like bread sponge in a pan, they began to rise, pushing the mother up so that she was forced to stand over them; then pushing her out until she could cling only to the side of the nest at night; then pushing her off altogether. By this time they were hanging to the outside themselves, covering the nest from sight almost, until finally they spilled off upon their wings.

Out of the nest upon the air! Out of the pen and into a sweet, wide world of green and blue and of golden light! I saw one of the broods take this first flight, and it was thrilling.

The nest was placed back from the window and below it, so that in leaving the nest the young would have to drop, then turn and fly up to get out. Below was the pig.

As they grew, I began to fear that they might try their wings before this feat could be accomplished, and so fall to the pig below. But Nature, in this case, was careful of her pearls. Day after day they clung to the nest, even after they might have flown; and when they did go, it was with a sure and long flight that carried them out and away to the tops of the neighboring trees.

They left the nest one at a time and were met in the air by their mother, who, darting to them, calling loudly, and, whirling about them, helped them as high and as far away as they could go.

I wish the simple record of these family affairs could be closed without one tragic entry. But that can rarely be of any family. Seven days after the first brood were awing, I found the new eggs in the nest. Soon after that the male bird disappeared. The second brood had now been out a week, and in all that time no sight or sound was had of the father.

What happened? Was he killed? Caught by a cat or a hawk? It is possible; and this is an easy and kindly way to think of him. It is not impossible that he may have remained as leader and protector to the first brood; or (perish the thought!) might he have grown weary at sight of the second lot of five eggs, of the long days and the neglect that they meant for him, and out of jealousy and fickleness wickedly deserted?

I hope it was death, a stainless, even ignominious death by one of my neighbor's many cats.

Death or desertion, it involved a second tragedy. Five such young ones at this time were too many for the mother. She fought nobly; no mother could have done more. All five were brought within a few days of flight; then, one day, I saw a little wing hanging listlessly over the side of the nest. I went closer. One had died. It had starved to death. There were none of the parasites in the nest that often kill whole broods. It was a plain case of sacrifice,—by the mother, perhaps; by the other young, maybe—one for the other four.

But she did well. Nine such young birds to her credit since April. Who shall measure her actual use to the world? How does she compare in value with the pig? Weeks later I saw several of her brood along the meadow fence hawking for flies. They were not far from my cabbage-patch.

14

I hope a pair of them will return to me next spring and that they will come early. Any bird that deigns to dwell under roof of mine commands my friendship. But no other bird takes Phœbe's place in my affections; there is so much in him to like, and he speaks for so much of the friendship of nature.

"Humble and inoffensive bird" he has been called by one of our leading ornithologies— because he comes to my pig-pen! Inoffensive! this bird with the cabbage butterfly in his beak! The faint and damning praise! And humble? There is not a humble feather on his body. Humble to those who see the pen and not the bird. But to me—why, the bird has made a palace of my pig-pen!

The very pig seems less a pig because of this exquisite association; and the lowly work of feeding the creature has been turned for me by Phœbe into a poetic course in bird study.

CHAPTER VIII
IS IT A LIFE OF FEAR?

THERE was a swish of wings, a flash of gray, a cry of pain; a squawking, cowering, scattering flock of hens; a weakly fluttering pullet; and yonder, swinging upward into the sky, a marsh hawk, buoyant and gleaming silvery in the sun. Over the trees he beat, circled once, and disappeared.

The hens were still flapping for safety in a dozen directions, but the gray harrier had gone. A bolt of lightning could hardly have dropped so unannounced, could hardly have vanished so completely, could scarcely have killed so quickly. I ran to the pullet, but found her dead. The harrier's stroke, delivered with fearful velocity, had laid head and neck open as with a keen knife. Yet a little slower and he would have missed, for the pullet warded off the other claw with her wing. The gripping talons slipped off the long quills, and the hawk swept on without his quarry. He dared not come back for it at my feet; so, with a single turn above the woods he was gone.

The scurrying hens stopped to look about them. There was nothing in the sky to see. They stood still and silent a moment. The rooster *chucked*. Then one by one they turned back into the open pasture. A huddled group under the hen-yard fence broke up and came out with the others. Death had flashed among them, but had missed *them*. Fear had come, but it had gone. Within two minutes from the fall of the stroke, every hen in the flock was intent at her scratching, or as intently chasing the gray grasshoppers over the pasture.

Yet, as the flock scratched, the high-stepping cock would frequently cast up his eye toward the tree-tops; would sound his alarum at the flight of a robin; and if a crow came over, he would shout and dodge and start to run. But instantly the shadow would pass, and instantly Chanticleer—

"He looketh as it were a grym leoun,
And on hise toos he rometh up and doun;

.   .   .   .

Thus roial as a prince is in an halle."

He wasn't afraid. Cautious, alert, watchful he was, but not afraid. No shadow of dread lay dark and ominous across the sunshine of his pasture. Shadows came—like a flash; and like a flash they vanished away.

We cannot go far into the fields without sighting the hawk and the snake, whose other names are Death. In one form or another Death moves everywhere, down every wood-path and pasture-lane, through the black waters of the mill-pond, out under the open of the April sky, night and day, and every day, the four seasons through.

I have seen the still surface of a pond break suddenly with a swirl, and flash a hundred flecks of silver into the light, as the minnows leap from the jaws of the terrible pike. Then a loud rattle, a streak of blue, a splash at the centre of the swirl, and I see the pike twisting and bending in the beak of the terrible kingfisher. The killer is killed. But at the mouth of the nest-hole in the steep sand-bank, swaying from a root in the edge of the turf above, hangs the terrible black snake, the third killer; and the belted kingfisher, dropping the pike, darts off with a startled cry.

I have been afield at times when one tragedy has followed another in such rapid and continuous succession as to put a whole shining, singing, blossoming springtime under a pall. Everything has seemed to cower, skulk, and hide, to run as if pursued. There was no peace, no stirring of small life, not even in the quiet of the deep pines; for here a hawk would be nesting, or a snake would be sleeping, or I would hear the passing of a fox, see perhaps his keen, hungry face an instant as he halted, winding me.

There is struggle, and pain, and death in the woods, and there is fear also, but the fear does not last long; it does not haunt and follow and terrify; it has no being, no shape, no lair. The shadow of the swiftest scudding cloud is not so fleeting as this Fear-shadow in the woods. The lowest of the animals seem capable of feeling fear; yet the very highest of them seem incapable of dreading it. For them Fear is not of the imagination, but of the sight, and of the passing moment.

"The present only toucheth thee!"

It does more, it throngs him—our little fellow mortal of the stubble-field. Into the present is lived the whole of his life—he remembers none of it; he anticipates none of it. And the whole of this life is action; and the whole of this action is joy. The moments of fear in an animal's life are few and vanishing. Action and joy are constant, the joint laws of all animal life, of all nature—of the shining stars that sing together, of the little mice that squeak together, of the bitter northeast storms that roar across the wintry fields.

I have had more than one hunter grip me excitedly, and with almost a command bid me hear the music of the baying pack. There are hollow halls in the swamps that lie to the east and north and west of me, that catch up the cry of the foxhounds, that blend it, mellow it, round it, and roll it, rising and falling over the meadows in great globes of sound, as pure and sweet as the pearly notes of the veery rolling round their silver basin in the summer dusk.

What music it is when the pack breaks into the open on the warm trail! A chorus then of tongues singing the ecstasy of pursuit! My blood leaps; the natural primitive wild thing of muscle and nerve and instinct within me slips its leash, and on past with the pack I drive, the scent of the trail single and sweet in my nostrils, a very fire in my blood, motion, motion, motion in my bounding muscles, and in my being a mighty music, spheric and immortal!

"The fair music that all creatures made
To their great Lord, whose love their motions swayed...."

But what about the fox, loping wearily on ahead? What part has he in the chorus? No part, perhaps, unless we grimly call him its conductor. But the point is the chorus—that it never ceases, the hounds at this moment, not the fox, in the leading rôle.

"But the chorus ceases for me," you say. "My heart is with the poor fox." So is mine, and mine is with the dogs too. No, don't say "Poor little fox!" For many a night I have bayed with the pack, and as often—oftener, I think—I have loped and dodged and doubled with the fox, pitting limb against limb, lung against lung, wit against wit, and always escaping.More than once, in the warm moonlight, I, the fox, have led them on and on, spurring their lagging muscles with a sight of my brush, on and on, through the moonlit night, through the day, on into the moon again, and on until—only the stir of my own footsteps has followed me. Then, doubling once more, creeping back a little upon my track, I have looked at my pursuers, silent and stiff upon the trail, and, ere the echo of their cry has died away, I have caught up the chorus and carried it single-throated through the wheeling, singing spheres.

There is more of fact than of fancy to this. That a fox ever purposely led a dog to run to death would be hard to prove; but that the dogs run themselves to death in a single extended chase after a single fox is a common occurrence here in the woods about the farm. Occasionally the fox may be overtaken by the hounds; seldom, however, except in the case of a very young one or of one unacquainted with the lay of the land, a stranger that may have been driven into the rough country here.

I have been both fox and hound; I have run the race too often not to know that both enjoy it at times, fox as much as hound. Some weeks ago the dogs carried a young fox around and around the farm, hunting him here, there, everywhere, as if in a game of hide-and-seek. An old fox would have led the dogs on a long coursing run across the range. But the young fox, after the dogs were caught and taken off the trail, soon sauntered up through the mowing-field behind the barn, came out upon the bare knoll near the house, and sat there in the moonlight yapping down at Rex and Dewey, the house-dogs in the two farms below. Rex is a Scotch collie, Dewey a dreadful mix of dog-dregs. He had been tail-ender in the pack for a while during the afternoon. Both dogs answered back at the young fox. But he could not egg them on. Rex was too fat, Dewey had had enough; not so the young fox. It had been fun. He wanted more. "Come on, Dewey!" he cried. "Come on, Rex, play tag again! You're still 'it.'"

I was at work with my chickens one spring day when the fox broke from cover in the tall woods, struck the old wagon-road along the ridge, and came at a gallop down behind the hen-coops, with five hounds not a minute behind. They passed with a crash and were gone—up over the ridge and down into the east swamp. Soon I noticed that the pack had broken, deploying in every direction, beating the ground over and over. Reynard had given them the slip—on the ridge-side, evidently, for there were no cries from below in the swamp.

Leaving my work at noon, I went down to restake my cow in the meadow. I had just drawn her chain-pin when down the road through the orchard behind me came the fox, hopping high up and down, his neck stretched, his eye peeled for poultry. Spying a white hen of my neighbor's, he made for her, clear to the barnyard wall. Then, hopping higher for a better view, he sighted another hen in the front yard, skipped in through the fence, seized her, and loped across the road and away up the birch-grown hills beyond.

The dogs had been at his very heels ten minutes before. He had fooled them. And no doubt he had done it again and again. They were even now yelping at the end of the baffling trail behind the ridge. Let them yelp. It is a kind and convenient habit of dogs, this yelping, one can tell so exactly where they are. Meantime one can take a turn for one's self at the chase, get a bite of chicken, a drink of water, a wink or two of rest, and when the yelping gets warm again, one is quite ready to pick up one's heels and lead the pack another merry dance. The fox is quite a jolly fellow.

This is the way the races out of doors are all run off. Now and then they may end tragically. A fox cannot reckon on the hunter with a gun. He is racing against the pack of hounds. But, mortal finish or no, the spirit of the chase is neither rage nor terror, but the excitement of a matched game, the ecstasy of pursuit for the hound, the passion of escape for the fox, without fury or fear—except for the instant at the start and at the finish—when it is a finish.

This is the spirit of the chase—of the race, more truly; for it is always a race, where the stake is not life and death, but rather the joy of winning. The hound cares as little for his own life as for the life of the fox he is hunting. It is the race, instead, that he loves; it is the moments of crowded, complete, supreme existence for him—"glory" we call it when men run it off together. Death, and the fear of death, the animals can neither understand nor feel. Only enemies exist in the world out of doors, only hounds, foxes, hawks—they, and their scents, their sounds and shadows; and not fear, but readiness only. The level of wild life, of the soul of all nature, is a great serenity. It is seldom lowered, but often raised to a higher level, intenser, faster, more exultant.

The serrate pines on my horizon are not the pickets of a great pen. My fields and swamps and ponds are not one wide battle-field, as if the only work of my wild neighbors were bloody war, and the whole of their existence a reign of terror. This is a universe of law and order and marvelous balance; conditions these of life, of normal, peaceful, joyous life. Life and not death is the law; joy and not fear is the spirit, is the frame of all that breathes, of very matter itself.

"And ever at the loom of Birth
The Mighty Mother weaves and sings;
She weaves—fresh robes for mangled earth;
She sings—fresh hopes for desperate things."

But suppose the fox were a defenseless rabbit, what of fear and terror then?

Ask any one who has shot in the rabbity fields of southern New Jersey. The rabbit seldom runs in blind terror. He is soft-eyed, and timid, and as gentle as a pigeon, but he is not defenseless. A nobler set of legs was never bestowed by nature than the little cottontail's. They are as wings compared with the bent, bow legs that bear up the ordinary rabbit-hound. With winged legs, protecting color, a clear map of the country in his head,—its stumps, railpiles, cat-brier tangles, and narrow rabbit-roads,—with all this as a handicap, Bunny may well run his usual cool and winning race. The balance is just as even, the chances quite as good, and the contest every bit as interesting to him as to Reynard.

I have seen a rabbit squat close in his form and let a hound pass yelping within a few feet of him, but waiting on his toes as ready as a hair-trigger should he be discovered.

I have seen him leap for his life as the dog sighted him, and, bounding like a ball across the stubble, disappear in the woods, the hound within two jumps of his flashing tail. I have waited at the end of the wood-road for the runners to come back, down the home-stretch, for the finish. On they go through the woods, for a quarter, or perhaps a half a mile, the baying of the hound faint and intermittent in the distance, then quite lost. No, there it is again, louder now. They have turned the course.

I wait.

The quiet life of the woods is undisturbed; for the voice of the hound is only an echo, not unlike the far-off tolling of a slow-swinging bell. The leaves stir as a wood mouse scurries from his stump; an acorn rattles down; then in the winding wood-road I hear the *pit-pat, pit-pat*, of soft furry feet, and there at the bend is the rabbit. He stops, rises high up on his haunches, and listens. He drops again upon all fours, scratches himself behind the ear, reaches over the cart-rut for a nip of sassafras, hops a little nearer, and throws his big ears forward in quick alarm, for he sees me, and, as if something had exploded under him, he kicks into the air and is off,—leaving a pretty tangle for the dog to unravel, later on, by this mighty jump to the side.

My children and a woodchopper were witnesses recently of an exciting, and, for this section of Massachusetts, a novel race, which, but for them, must certainly have ended fatally. The boys were coming through the wood-lot where the man was chopping, when down the hillside toward them rushed a little chipmunk, his teeth a-chatter with terror; for close behind him, with the easy, wavy motion of a shadow, glided a dark-brown animal, which the man took on the instant for a mink, but which must have been a large weasel or a pine marten. When almost at the feet of the boys, and about to be seized by the marten, the squeaking chipmunk ran up a tree. Up glided the marten, up for twenty feet, when the chipmunk jumped. It was a fearfully close call.

The marten did not dare to jump, but turned and started down, when the man intercepted him with a stick. Around and around the tree he dodged, growling and snarling and avoiding the stick, not a bit abashed, stubbornly holding his own, until forced to seek refuge among the branches. Meanwhile, the terrified chipmunk had recovered his nerve and sat quietly watching the sudden turn of affairs from a near-by stump.

I frequently climb into the cupola of the barn during the winter, and bring down a dazed junco that would beat his life out up there against the window-panes. He will lie on his back in my open hand, either feigning death or really powerless with fear. His eyes will close, his whole tiny body throb convulsively with his throbbing heart. Taking him to the door, I will turn him over and give him a gentle toss. Instantly his wings flash; they take him zigzag for a yard or two, then bear him swiftly round the corner of the house and drop him in the midst of his fellows, where they are feeding upon the lawn. He will shape himself up a little and fall to picking with the others.

From a state of collapse the laws of his being bring the bird into normal behavior as quickly and completely as the collapsed rubber ball is rounded by the laws of its being. The memory of the fright seems to be an impression exactly like the dent in the rubber ball—as if it had never been.

Memories, of course, the animals surely have; but little or no power to use them. The dog will sometimes seem to cherish a grudge; so will the elephant. Some one injures or wrongs him, and the huge beast harbors the memory, broods it, and awaits his opportunity for revenge. Yet the records of these cases usually show that the creature had been living with the object of his hatred—his keeper, perhaps—and that the memory goes no farther back than the present moment, than the sight of the hated one.

At my railroad station I frequently see a yoke of great sleepy, bald-faced oxen, that look as much alike as two blackbirds. Their driver knows them apart; but as they stand there, bound to one another by the heavy bar across their foreheads, it would puzzle anybody else to tell Buck from Berry. But not if he approach them wearing an overcoat. At sight of me in an overcoat the off ox will snort and back and thrash about in terror, twisting the head of his yoke-fellow, nearly breaking his neck, and trampling him miserably. But the nigh ox is used to it. He chews and blinks away placidly, keeps his feet the best he can, and doesn't try to understand at all why greatcoats should so frighten his cud-chewing brother. I will drop off my coat and go up immediately to smooth the muzzles of both oxen, now blinking sleepily while the lumber is being loaded on.

Years ago, the driver told me, the off ox was badly frightened by a big woolly coat, the sight or smell of which probably suggested to the creature some natural enemy, a panther, perhaps, or a bear. The memory remained, but beyond recall except in the presence of its first cause, the greatcoat.

To us there are such things as terror and death, but not to the lower animals except momentarily. We are clutched by terror even as the junco was clutched in my goblin hand. When the mighty fingers open, we zigzag, dazed, from the danger; but fall to planning before the tremors of the fright have ceased. Upon the crumbled, smoking heap of San Francisco a second splendid city has arisen and shall ever rise. Terror can kill the living, but it cannot hinder them from forgetting, or prevent them from hoping, or, for more than an instant, stop them from doing. Such is the law of life—the law of heaven, of my pastures, of the little junco, of myself. Life, Law, and Matter are all of one piece. The horse in my stable, the robin, the toad, the beetle, the vine in my garden, the garden itself, and I together with them all, come out of the same divine dust; we all breathe the same divine breath; we have our beings under the same divine laws; only they do not know that the law, the breath, and the dust are divine. If, with all that I know of fear, I can so readily forget it, and can so constantly feel the hope and the joy of life within me, how soon for them, my lowly fellow mortals, must vanish all sight of fear, all memory of pain! And how abiding with them, how compelling, the necessity to live! And in their unquestioning obedience, what joy!

The face of the fields is as changeful as the face of a child. Every passing wind, every shifting cloud, every calling bird, every baying hound, every shape, shadow, fragrance, sound, and tremor, are reflected there. But if time and experience and pain come, they pass utterly away; for the face of the fields does not grow old or wise or seamed with pain. It is always the face of a child,—asleep in winter, awake in spring and summer,—a face of life and health always, as much in the falling leaf as in the opening bud, as much under the covers of the snow as in the greensward of the spring, as much in the wild, fierce joy of fox and hound as they course the turning, tangling paths of the woodlands in their fateful race as in the song of brook and bird on a joyous April morning.

CHAPTER IX
THE BUZZARD OF THE BEAR SWAMP

NO, I do not believe that any one of you ever went into a swamp to find a turkey buzzard's nest. Still, if you had been born on the edge of a great swamp, as I was, and if the great-winged buzzards had been soaring, soaring up in your sky, as all through my boyhood they were soaring up in mine, then why should you not have gone some time into the swamp to see where they make their nests—these strange cloud-winged creatures?

Boys are boys, and girls are girls, the world over; and I am pretty sure that little Jack Horner and myself were not the only two boys in all the world to do great and wonderful deeds. Any boy with a love for birds and a longing for the deep woods, living close to the edge of the Bear Swamp, would have searched out that buzzard's nest.

Although I was born within the shadows of the Bear Swamp, close enough to smell the magnolias along its margin, and lived my first ten years only a little farther off, yet it was not until after twice ten years of absence that I stood again within sight of it, ready for the first time to cross its dark borders and find the buzzard's nest.

Now here at last I found myself, looking down over the largest, least trod, deepest-tangled swamp in southern New Jersey—wide, gloomy, silent, and to me,—for I still thought of it as I used to when a child,—to me, a mysterious realm of black streams, hollow trees, animal trails, and haunting shapes, presided over by this great bird, the turkey buzzard.

For he was never mere bird to me, but some kind of spirit. He stood to me for what was far off, mysterious, secret, and unapproachable in the deep, dark swamp; and, in the sky, so wide were his wings, so majestic the sweep of his flight, he had always stirred me, caused me to hold my breath and wish myself to fly.

No other bird did I so much miss from my New England skies when I came here to live. Only the other day, standing in the heart of Boston, I glanced up and saw, sailing at a far height against the billowy clouds, an aeroplane; and what should I think of but the flight of the vulture, so like the steady wings of the great bird seemed the steady wings of this great monoplane far off against the sky.

And so you begin to understand why I had come back after so many years to the swamp, and why I wanted to see the nest of this strange bird that had been flying, flying forever in my imagination and in my sky. But my good uncle, whom I was visiting, when I mentioned my quest, merely exclaimed, "What in thunderation!"

You will find a good many uncles and other folk who won't understand a good many things that you want to do. Never mind. If you want to see a buzzard's nest, let all your relations exclaim while you go quietly off alone and see it.

I wanted to find a buzzard's nest—the nest of the Bear Swamp buzzard; and here at last I stood; and yonder on the clouds, a mere mote in the distance, floated the bird. It was coming toward me over the wide reach of the swamp.

Silent, inscrutable, and alien lay the swamp, and untouched by human hands. Over it spread a quiet and reserve as real as twilight. Like a mask it was worn, and was slipped on, I know, at my approach. I could feel the silent spirit of the place drawing back away from me. But I should have at least a guide to lead me through the shadow land, for out of the lower living green towered a line of limbless stubs, like a line of telegraph-poles, their bleached bones gleaming white, or showing dark and gaunt against the horizon, and marking for me a path far out across the swamp. Besides, here came the buzzard winding slowly down the clouds. Soon its spiral changed to a long pendulum-swing, till just above the skeleton trees the great bird wheeled and, bracing itself with its flapping wings, dropped heavily upon one of the headless tree-trunks.

It had come leisurely, yet I could see that it had come with a directness and purpose that was unmistakable and also meaningful. It had discovered me in the distance, and, while still invisible to my eyes, had started down to perch upon that giant stub in order to watch me. It was suspicious, and had come to watch me, because somewhere beneath its perch, I felt sure, lay a hollow log, the creature's den, holding its two eggs or its young. A buzzard has something like a soul.

Marking the direction of the stub, and its probable distance, I waded into the deep underbrush, the buzzard perched against the sky for my guide, and, for my quest, the stump or hollow log that held the creature's nest.

19

The rank ferns and ropy vines swallowed me up, and shut out at times even the sight of the sky and the buzzard. It was not until half an hour's struggle that, climbing a pine-crested swell in the low bottom, I sighted the bird again. It had not moved.

I was now in the real swamp, the old uncut forest. It was a land of tree giants: huge tulip poplar and swamp white oak, so old that they had become solitary, their comrades having fallen one by one; while some of them, unable to loose their grip upon the soil, which had widened and tightened through centuries, were still standing, though long since dead. It was upon one of these that the buzzard sat humped.

Directly in my path stood an ancient swamp white oak, the greatest tree, I think, that I have ever seen. It was not the highest, nor the largest round, perhaps, but in years and looks the greatest. Hoary, hollow, and broken-limbed, his huge bole seemed encircled with the centuries.

"For it had bene an auncient tree,
Sacred with many a mysteree."

Above him to twice his height loomed a tulip poplar, clean-boled for thirty feet and in the top all green and gold with blossoms. It was a resplendent thing beside the oak, yet how unmistakably the gnarled old monarch wore the crown! His girth more than balanced the poplar's greater height; and, as for blossoms, he had his tiny-flowered catkins; but nature knows the beauty of strength and inward majesty, and has pinned no boutonnière upon the oak.

My buzzard now was hardly more than half a mile away, and plainly seen through the rifts in the lofty timbered roof above me. As I was nearing the top of a large fallen pine that lay in my course, I was startled by the *burrh! burrh! burrh!* of three partridges taking wing just beyond, near the foot of the tree. Their exploding flight seemed all the more like a real explosion when three little clouds of dust-smoke rose out of the low, *wet* bottom of the swamp and drifted up against the green.

Then I saw an interesting sight. The pine, in its fall, had snatched with its wide-reaching, multitudinous roots at the shallow bottom and torn out a giant fistful of earth, leaving a hole about two feet deep and more than a dozen feet wide. The sand thus lifted into the air had gradually washed down into a mound on each side of the butt, where it lay high and dry above the level of the wet swamp. This the swamp birds had turned into a great dust-bath. It was in constant use, evidently. Not a spear of grass had sprouted in it, and all over it were pits and craters of various sizes, showing that not only the partridges but also the quail and such small things as the warblers bathed here,—though I can't recall ever having seen a warbler bathe in the dust. A dry bath in the swamp was something of a luxury, evidently. I wonder if the buzzards used it?

I went forward cautiously now, and expectantly, for I was close enough to see the white beak and red wattled neck of my buzzard guide. The buzzard saw me, too, and began to twist its head and to twitch its wing-tips nervously. Then the long, black wings began to open, as you would open a two-foot rule, and, with a heavy lurch that left the dead stub rocking, the bird dropped and was soon soaring high up in the blue.

This was the locality of the nest; now where should I find it? Evidently I was to have no further help from the old bird. The underbrush was so thick that I could hardly see farther than my nose. A half-rotten tree-trunk lay near, the top end resting across the backs of several saplings that it had borne down in its fall. I crept up on this for a look around, and almost tumbled off at finding myself staring directly into the dark, cavernous hollow of an immense log lying on a slight rise of ground a few feet ahead of me.

It was a yawning hole, which at a glance I knew belonged to the buzzard. The log, a mere shell of a mighty white oak, had been girdled and felled with an axe, by coon-hunters probably, and still lay with one side resting upon the rim of the stump. As I stood looking, something white stirred vaguely in the hole and disappeared.

Leaping from my perch, I scrambled forward to the mouth of the hollow log and was greeted with hisses from far back in the dark. Then came a thumping of bare feet, more hisses, and a sound of snapping beaks. I had found my buzzard's nest!

YOUNG TURKEY BUZZARD

Hardly that, either, for there was not a feather, stick, or chip as evidence of a nest. The eggs had been laid upon the sloping cavern floor, and in the course of their incubation must have rolled clear down to the opposite end, where the opening was so narrow that the buzzard could not have brooded them until she had rolled them back. The wonder is that they had ever hatched.

But they had, and what they hatched was another wonder. Nature never intended a young buzzard for any eye but his mother's, and *she* hates the sight of him. Elsewhere I have told of a buzzard that devoured her eggs at the approach of an enemy, so delicately balanced are her unnamable appetites and her maternal affections!

The two strange nestlings in the log must have been three weeks old, I should say, the larger weighing about four pounds. They were covered, as young owls are, with deep snow-white down, out of which protruded their black scaly, snaky legs. They stood braced on these long black legs, their receding heads drawn back, shoulders thrust forward, and bodies humped between the featherless wings like challenging tom-cats.

In order to examine them, I crawled into the den—not a difficult act, for the opening measured four feet and a half across at the mouth. The air was musty inside, yet surprisingly free from odor. The floor was absolutely clean, but on the top and sides of the cavity was a thick coating of live mosquitoes, most of them gorged, hanging like a red-beaded tapestry over the walls.

I had taken pains that the flying buzzard should not see me enter, for I hoped she would descend to look after her young. But she would take no chances with herself. I sat near the mouth of the hollow, where I could catch the fresh breeze that pulled across the end, and where I had a view of a far-away bit of sky. Suddenly, across this field of blue, there swept a meteor of black—the buzzard! and evidently in that instant of passage, at a distance certainly of half a mile, she spied me in the log.

I waited more than an hour longer, and when I tumbled out with a dozen kinds of cramps, the unworried mother was soaring serenely far up in the clear, cool sky.

CHAPTER X
A CHAPTER OF THINGS TO HEAR THIS SPRING
I

THE frogs! You can have no spring until you hear the frogs. The first shrill notes, heard before the ice is fairly out of the marshes, will be the waking call of the hylas, the tiny tree-frogs that later on in the summer you will find in the woods. Then, as the spring advances and this silvery sleigh-bell jingle tinkles faster, other voices will join in—the soft croak of the spotted leopard frogs, the still softer melancholy quaver of the common toad, and away down at the end of the scale the deep, solemn bass of the great bullfrog saying, "Go round! Better go round!"

II

You must hear, besides the first spring notes of the bluebird and the robin, four bird songs this spring. First (1) the song of the wood thrush or the hermit thrush, whichever one lives in your neighborhood. No words can describe the purity, the peacefulness, the spiritual quality of the wood thrush's simple "Come to me." It is the voice of the tender twilight, the voice of the tranquil forest, speaking to you. After the thrush (2) the brown thrasher, our finest, most gifted songster, as great a singer, I think (and I have often heard them both), as the Southern mockingbird. Then (3) the operatic catbird. She sits lower down among the bushes than the brown thrasher, as if she knew that, compared with him, she must take a back seat; but for variety of notes and length of song, she has few rivals. I say *she*, when really I ought to say *he*, for it is the males of most birds that sing, but the catbird seems so long and slender, so dainty and feminine, that I think of this singer as of some exquisite operatic singer in a woman's rôle. Then (4) the bobolink; for his song is just like Bryant's bubbling poem, only better! Go to the meadows in June and listen as he comes lilting and singing over your head.

III

There are some birds that cannot sing: the belted kingfisher, for instance; he can only rattle. You must hear him rattle. You can do as well yourself if you will shake a "pair of bones" or heave an anchor and let the chain run fast through the hawse-hole. You then must hear the downy woodpecker doing his rattling *rat-ta-tat-tat-tat-tat* (across the page and back again), as fast as *rat-ta-tat* can *tat*. How he makes the old dead limb or fence-post rattle as he drums upon it with his chisel bill. He can be heard half a mile around.

Then high-hole, the flicker (or golden-winged woodpecker), you must hear him yell, *Up-up-up-up-up up-up-up-up-up-up*,—a ringing, rolling, rapid kind of yodel that echoes over the spring fields.

IV

You must hear the nighthawk and the whip-poor-will. Both birds are to be heard at twilight, and the whip-poor-will far into the night. At the very break of dawn is also a good time to listen to them.

At dusk you will see (I have seen him from the city roofs in Boston) a bird about the size of a pigeon mounting up into the sky by short flights, crying *peent*, until far over your head the

21

creature will suddenly turn and on half-closed wings dive headlong toward the earth, when, just before hitting the ground, upward he swoops, at the same instant making a weird booming sound, a kind of hollow groan with his wings, as the wind rushes through their large feathers. This diver through the dim ocean of air is the nighthawk. Let one of the birds dive close to your head on a lonely dusky road, and your hair will try to jump out from under your hat.

The whip-poor-will's cry you all know. When you hear one this spring, go out into the twilight and watch for him. See him spring into the air, like a strange shadow, for flies; count his *whip-poor-wills* (he may call it more than a hundred times in as many seconds!). But hear a circle of the birds, if possible, calling through the darkness of a wood all around you!

V

There is one strange bird song that is half song and half dance that perhaps most of you may never be able to hear and see; but as it is worth going miles to hear, and nights of watching to witness, I am going to set it here as one of your outdoor tasks or feats: you must hear the mating song of the woodcock. I have described the song and the dance in "Roof and Meadow," in the chapter called "One Flew East and One Flew West." Mr. Bradford Torrey has an account of it in his "Clerk of the Woods," in the chapter named "Woodcock Vespers." To hear the song is a rare experience for the habitual watcher in the woods, but one that you might have the first April evening that you are abroad.

Go down to your nearest meadow—a meadow near a swampy piece of woods is best—and here, along the bank of the meadow stream, wait in the chilly twilight for the *speank, speank*, or the *peent, peent*, from the grass—the signal that the song is about to begin.

VI

One of the dreadful—positively dreadful—sounds of the late spring that I hear day in and day out is the gobbling, strangling, ghastly cries of young crows feeding. You will surely think something is being murdered. The crying of a hungry baby is musical in comparison. But it is a good sound to hear, for it reminds one of the babes in the woods—that a new generation of birds is being brought through from babyhood to gladden the world. It is a tender sound! The year is still young.

VII

You should hear the hum of the honey-bees on a fresh May day in an apple tree that is just coming into perfect bloom. The enchanting loveless of the pink and white world of blossoms is enough to make one forget to listen to the *hum-hum-hum-humming-ing-ing-ing-ing* of the excited bees. But hear their myriad wings, fanning the perfume into the air and filling the sunshine with the music of work. The whir, the hum of labor—of a busy factory, of a great steamship dock—is always music to those who know the blessedness of work; but it takes that knowledge, and a good deal of imagination besides, to hear the music in it. Not so with the bees. The season, the day, the colors, and perfumes—they are the song; the wings are only the million-stringed æolian upon which the song is played.

VIII

You should hear the grass grow. What! I repeat, you should hear the grass grow. I have a friend, a sound and sensible man, but a lover of the out-of-doors, who says he can hear it grow. But perhaps it is the soft stir of the working earthworms that he hears. Try it. Go out alone one of these April nights; select a green pasture with a slope to the south, at least a mile from any house, or railroad; lay your ear flat upon the grass, listen without a move for ten minutes. You hear something—or do you feel it? Is it the reaching up of the grass? is it the stir of the earthworms? is it the pulse of the throbbing universe? or is it your own throbbing pulse? It is all of these, I think; call it the heart of the grass beating in every tiny living blade, if you wish to. You should listen to hear the grass grow.

IX

The fires have gone out on the open hearth. Listen early in the morning and toward evening for the rumbling, the small, muffled thunder, of the chimney swallows, as they come down from the open sky on their wonderful wings. Don't be frightened. It isn't Santa Claus this time of year; nor is it the Old Nick! The smothered thunder is caused by the rapid beating of the swallows' wings on the air in the narrow chimney-flue, as the birds settle down from the top of the chimney and hover over their nests. Stick your head into the fireplace and look up! Don't smoke the precious lodgers out, no matter how much racket they make.

X

Hurry out while the last drops of your first May thunder-shower are still falling and listen to the robins singing from the tops of the trees. Their liquid songs are as fresh as the shower, as if the raindrops in falling were running down from the trees in song—as indeed they are in the overflowing trout-brook. Go out and listen, and write a better poem than this one that I wrote the other afternoon when listening to the birds in our first spring shower:—

22

The warm rain drops aslant the sun
And in the rain the robins sing;
Across the creek in twos and troops,
The hawking swifts and swallows wing.
The air is sweet with apple bloom,
And sweet the laid dust down the lane,
The meadow's marge of calamus,
And sweet the robins in the rain.
O greening time of bloom and song!
O fragrant days of tender pain!
The wet, the warm, the sweet young days
With robins singing in the rain.

CHAPTER XI
TURTLE EGGS FOR AGASSIZ

I TOOK down, recently, from the shelves of a great public library, the four volumes of Agassiz's "Contributions to the Natural History of the United States." I doubt if anybody but the charwoman, with her duster, had touched those volumes for twenty-five years. They are a monumental work, the fruit of vast and heroic labors, with colored plates on stone, showing the turtles of the United States, and their life-history. The work was published more than half a century ago, but it looked old beyond its years—massive, heavy, weathered, as if dug from the rocks; and I soon turned with a sigh from the weary learning of its plates and diagrams to look at the preface.

Then, reading down through the catalogue of human names and of thanks for help received, I came to a sentence beginning:—

"In New England I have myself collected largely; but I have also received valuable contributions from the late Rev. Zadoc Thompson of Burlington; ... from Mr. D. Henry Thoreau of Concord; ... and from Mr. J. W. P. Jenks of Middleboro." And then it hastens on with the thanks in order to get to the turtles, as if turtles were the one and only thing of real importance in all the world.

Turtles are important—interesting; so is the late Rev. Zadoc Thompson of Burlington. Indeed any reverend gentleman who would catch turtles for Agassiz must have been interesting. If Agassiz had only put a chapter into his turtle book about him! and as for the Mr. Jenks of Middleboro (at the end of the quotation) I know that he was interesting; for years later, he was an old college professor of mine. He told me some of the particulars of his turtle contributions, particulars which Agassiz should have found a place for in his big book. The preface says merely that this gentleman sent turtles to Cambridge by the thousands—brief and scanty recognition. For that is not the only thing this gentleman did. On one occasion he sent, not turtles, but turtle *eggs* to Cambridge—*brought* them, I should say; and all there is to show for it, so far as I could discover, is a small drawing of a bit of one of the eggs!

Of course, Agassiz wanted to make that drawing, and had to have a *fresh* turtle egg to draw it from. He had to have it, and he got it. A great man, when he wants a certain turtle egg, at a certain time, always gets it, for he gets some one else to get it for him. I am glad he got it. But what makes me sad and impatient is that he did not think it worth while to tell us about the getting of it.

It would seem, naturally, that there could be nothing unusual or interesting about the getting of turtle eggs when you want them. Nothing at all, if you should chance to want the eggs as you chance to find them. So with anything else. But if you want turtle eggs *when* you want them, and are bound to have them, then you must—get Mr. Jenks, or somebody else to get them for you.

Agassiz wanted those turtle eggs when he wanted them—not a minute over three hours from the minute they were laid. Yet even that does not seem exacting, hardly more difficult than the getting of hens' eggs only three hours old. Just so, provided the professor could have had his private turtle-coop in Harvard College Yard; and provided he could have made his turtles lay. But turtles will not respond, like hens, to meat-scraps and the warm mash. The professor's problem was not to get from a mud turtle's nest in the back yard to his work-table in the laboratory; but to get from the laboratory in Cambridge to some pond when the turtles were laying, and back to the laboratory within the limited time. And this might have called for nice and discriminating work—as it did.

Agassiz had been engaged for a long time upon his "Contributions." He had brought the great work nearly to a finish. It was, indeed, finished but for one small yet very important bit of observation: he had carried the turtle egg through every stage of its development with the single

23

exception of one—the very earliest. That beginning stage had brought the "Contributions" to a halt. To get eggs that were fresh enough to show the incubation at this period had been impossible.

There were several ways that Agassiz might have proceeded: he might have got a leave of absence for the spring term, taken his laboratory to some pond inhabited by turtles, and there camped until he should catch the reptile digging out her nest. But there were difficulties in all of that—as those who are college professors and naturalists know. As this was quite out of the question, he did the easiest thing—asked Mr. Jenks of Middleboro to get him the eggs. Mr. Jenks got them. Agassiz knew all about his getting of them; and I say the strange and irritating thing is, that Agassiz did not think it worth while to tell us about it, at least in the preface to his monumental work.

It was many years later that Mr. Jenks, then a gray-haired college professor, told me how he got those eggs to Agassiz.

"I was principal of an academy, during my younger years," he began, "and was busy one day with my classes, when a large man suddenly filled the doorway of the room, smiled to the four corners of the room, and called out with a big, quick voice that he was Professor Agassiz.

"Of course he was. I knew it, even before he had had time to shout it to me across the room.

"Would I get him some turtle eggs? he called. Yes, I would. And would I get them to Cambridge within three hours from the time they were laid? Yes, I would. And I did. And it was worth the doing. But I did it only once.

"When I promised Agassiz those eggs, I knew where I was going to get them. I had got turtle eggs there before—at a particular patch of sandy shore along a pond, a few miles distant from the academy.

"Three hours was the limit. From the railroad station to Boston was thirty-five miles; from the pond to the station was perhaps three or four miles; from Boston to Cambridge we called about three miles. Forty miles in round numbers! We figured it all out before he returned, and got the trip down to two hours,—record time:—driving from the pond to the station; from the station by express train to Boston; from Boston by cab to Cambridge. This left an easy hour for accidents and delays.

"Cab and car and carriage we reckoned into our time-table; but what we didn't figure on was the turtle." And he paused abruptly.

"Young man," he went on, his shaggy brows and spectacles hardly hiding the twinkle in the eyes that were bent severely upon me, "young man, when *you* go after turtle eggs, take into account the turtle. No! No! that's bad advice. Youth never reckons on the turtle—and youth seldom ought to. Only old age does that; and old age would never have got those turtle eggs to Agassiz.

"It was in the early spring that Agassiz came to the academy, long before there was any likelihood of the turtles' laying. But I was eager for the quest, and so fearful of failure that I started out to watch at the pond, fully two weeks ahead of the time that the turtles might be expected to lay. I remember the date clearly: it was May 14th.

"A little before dawn—along near three o'clock—I would drive over to the pond, hitch my horse near by, settle myself quietly among some thick cedars close to the sandy shore, and there I would wait, my kettle of sand ready, my eye covering the whole sleeping pond. Here among the cedars I would eat my breakfast, and then get back in good season to open the academy for the morning session.

"And so the watch began.

"I soon came to know individually the dozen or more turtles that kept to my side of the pond. Shortly after the cold mist would lift and melt away, they would stick up their heads through the quiet water; and as the sun slanted down over the ragged rim of tree-tops, the slow things would float into the warm lighted spots, or crawl out and doze comfortably on the hummocks and snags.

"What fragrant mornings those were! How fresh and new and unbreathed! The pond odors, the woods odors, the odors of the ploughed fields—of water-lily, and wild grape, and the dew-laid soil! I can taste them yet, and hear them yet—the still, large sounds of the waking day— the pickerel breaking the quiet with his swirl; the kingfisher dropping anchor; the stir of feet and wings among the trees. And then the thought of the great book being held up for me! Those were rare mornings!

"But there began to be a good many of them, for the turtles showed no desire to lay. They sprawled in the sun, and never one came out upon the sand as if she intended to help on the great professor's book. The story of her eggs was of small concern to her; her contribution to the Natural History of the United States could wait.

"And it did wait. I began my watch on the 14th of May; June 1st found me still among the cedars, still waiting, as I had waited every morning, Sundays and rainy days alike. June 1st was a perfect morning, but every turtle slid out upon her log, as if egg-laying might be a matter strictly of next year.

"I began to grow uneasy,—not impatient yet, for a naturalist learns his lesson of patience early, and for all his years; but I began to fear lest, by some subtle sense, my presence might somehow be known to the creatures; that they might have gone to some other place to lay, while I was away at the schoolroom.

"I watched on to the end of the first week, on to the end of the second week in June, seeing the mists rise and vanish every morning, and along with them vanish, more and more, the poetry of my early morning vigil. Poetry and rheumatism cannot long dwell together in the same clump of cedars, and I had begun to feel the rheumatism. A month of morning mists wrapping me around had at last soaked through to my bones. But Agassiz was waiting, and the world was waiting, for those turtle eggs and I would wait. It was all I could do, for there is no use bringing a china nest-egg to a turtle; she is not open to any such delicate suggestion.

"Then came a mid-June Sunday morning, with dawn breaking a little after three: a warm, wide-awake dawn, with the level mist lifted from the level surface of the pond a full hour higher than I had seen it any morning before.

"This was the day. I knew it. I have heard persons say that they can hear the grass grow; that they know by some extra sense when danger is nigh. For a month I had been watching, had been brooding over this pond, and now I knew. I felt a stirring of the pulse of things that the cold-hearted turtles could no more escape than could the clods and I.

"Leaving my horse unhitched, as if he, too, understood, I slipped eagerly into my covert for a look at the pond. As I did so, a large pickerel ploughed a furrow out through the spatter-docks, and in his wake rose the head of a large painted turtle. Swinging slowly round, the creature headed straight for the shore, and, without a pause, scrambled out on the sand.

"She was nothing unusual for a turtle, but her manner was unusual and the gait at which she moved; for there was method in it and fixed purpose. On she came, shuffling over the sand toward the higher open fields, with a hurried, determined see-saw that was taking her somewhere in particular, and that was bound to get her there on time.

"I held my breath. Had she been a dinosaurian making Mesozoic footprints, I could not have been more fearful. For footprints in the Mesozoic mud, or in the sands of time, were as nothing to me when compared with fresh turtle eggs in the sands of this pond.

"But over the strip of sand, without a stop, she paddled, and up a narrow cow-path into the high grass along a fence. Then up the narrow cow-path, on all fours, just like another turtle, I paddled, and into the high wet grass along the fence.

"I kept well within sound of her, for she moved recklessly, leaving a wide trail of flattened grass behind. I wanted to stand up,—and I don't believe I could have turned her back with a rail,—but I was afraid if she saw me that she might return indefinitely to the pond; so on I went, flat to the ground, squeezing through the lower rails of the fence, as if the field beyond were a melon-patch. It was nothing of the kind, only a wild, uncomfortable pasture, full of dewberry vines, and very discouraging. They were excessively wet vines and briery. I pulled my coat-sleeves as far over my fists as I could get them, and with the tin pail of sand swinging from between my teeth to avoid noise, I stumped fiercely, but silently, on after the turtle.

"TAIL FIRST, BEGAN TO BURY HERSELF"

"She was laying her course, I thought, straight down the length of this dreadful pasture, when, not far from the fence, she suddenly hove to, warped herself short about, and came back, barely clearing me. I warped about, too, and in her wake bore down across the corner of the pasture, across the powdery public road, and on to a fence along a field of young corn.

"I was somewhat wet by this time, but not so wet as I had been before wallowing through the deep, dry dust of the road. Hurrying up behind a large tree by the fence, I peered down the corn-rows and saw the turtle stop, and begin to paw about in the loose, soft soil. She was going to lay!

"I held on to the tree and watched, as she tried this place, and that place, and the other place. But *the* place, evidently, was hard to find. What could a female turtle do with a whole field of possible nests to choose from? Then at last she found it, and, whirling about, she backed quickly at it and, tail first, began to bury herself before my staring eyes.

"Those were not the supreme moments of my life; perhaps those moments came later that day; but those certainly were among the slowest, most dreadfully mixed of moments that I ever experienced. They were hours long. There she was, her shell just showing, like some old hulk in

25

the sand alongshore. And how long would she stay there? and how should I know if she had laid an egg?

"I could still wait. And so I waited, when, over the freshly awakened fields, floated four mellow strokes from the distant town clock.

"Four o'clock! Why there was no train until seven! No train for three hours! The eggs would spoil! Then with a rush it came over me that this was Sunday morning, and there was no regular seven o'clock train,—none till after nine.

"I think I should have fainted had not the turtle just then begun crawling off. I was weak and dizzy; but there, there in the sand, were the eggs! and Agassiz! and the great book! Why, I cleared the fence—and the forty miles that lay between me and Cambridge—at a single jump! He should have them, trains or no. Those eggs should go to Agassiz by seven o'clock, if I had to gallop every mile of the way. Forty miles! Any horse could cover it in three hours, if he had to; and, upsetting the astonished turtle, I scooped out her long white eggs.

"On a bed of sand in the bottom of the pail I laid them, with what care my trembling fingers allowed; filled in between them with more sand; so with layer after layer to the rim; and covering all smoothly with more sand, I ran back for my horse.

"That horse knew, as well as I, that the turtles had laid, and that he was to get those eggs to Agassiz. He turned out of that field into the road on two wheels, a thing he had not done for twenty years, doubling me up before the dashboard, the pail of eggs miraculously lodged between my knees.

"I let him out. If only he could keep this pace all the way to Cambridge!—or even halfway there, I would have time to finish the trip on foot. I shouted him on, holding to the dasher with one hand, holding the pail of eggs with the other, not daring to get off my knees, though the bang on them, as we pounded down the wood-road, was terrific. But nothing must happen to the eggs; they must not be jarred, or even turned over in the sand before they came to Agassiz.

"In order to get out on the pike it was necessary to drive back away from Boston toward the town. We had nearly covered the distance, and were rounding a turn from the woods into the open fields, when, ahead of me, at the station it seemed, I heard the quick, sharp whistle of a locomotive.

"What did it mean? Then followed the *puff, puff, puff,* of a starting train. But what train? Which way going? And jumping to my feet for a longer view, I pulled into a side road that paralleled the track, and headed hard for the station.

"We reeled along. The station was still out of sight, but from behind the bushes that shut it from view, rose the smoke of a moving engine. It was perhaps a mile away, but we were approaching, head on, and, topping a little hill, I swept down upon a freight train, the black smoke pouring from the stack, as the mighty creature pulled itself together for its swift run down the rails.

"My horse was on the gallop, following the track, and going straight toward the coming train. The sight of it almost maddened me—the bare thought of it, on the road to Boston! On I went; on it came, a half—a quarter of a mile between us, when suddenly my road shot out along an unfenced field with only a level stretch of sod between me and the engine.

"With a pull that lifted the horse from his feet, I swung him into the field and sent him straight as an arrow for the track. That train should carry me and my eggs to Boston!

"The engineer pulled the whistle. He saw me stand up in the rig, saw my hat blow off, saw me wave my arms, saw the tin pail swing in my teeth, and he jerked out a succession of sharp Halts! But it was he who should halt, not I; and on we went, the horse with a flounder landing the carriage on top of the track.

"The train was already grinding to a stop; but before it was near a standstill, I had backed off the track, jumped out, and, running down the rails with the astonished engineers gaping at me, had swung aboard the cab.

"They offered no resistance; they hadn't had time. Nor did they have the disposition, for I looked strange, not to say dangerous. Hatless, dew-soaked, smeared with yellow mud, and holding, as if it were a baby or a bomb, a little tin pail of sand!

"'Crazy,' the fireman muttered, looking to the engineer for his cue.

"I had been crazy, perhaps, but I was not crazy now.

"'Throw her wide open,' I commanded. 'Wide open! These are fresh turtle eggs for Professor Agassiz of Cambridge. He must have them before breakfast.'

"Then they knew I was crazy, and, evidently thinking it best to humor me, threw the throttle wide open, and away we went.

"I kissed my hand to the horse, grazing unconcernedly in the open field, and gave a smile to my crew. That was all I could give them, and hold myself and the eggs together. But the smile was enough. And they smiled through their smut at me, though one of them held fast to his shovel, while the other kept his hand upon a big ugly wrench. Neither of them spoke to me, but above the roar of the swaying engine I caught enough of their broken talk to understand that they were driving under a full head of steam, with the intention of handing me over to the Boston police, as perhaps the safest way of disposing of me.

"I was only afraid that they would try it at the next station. But that station whizzed past without a bit of slack, and the next, and the next; when it came over me that this was the through freight, which should have passed in the night, and was making up lost time.

"Only the fear of the shovel and the wrench kept me from shaking hands with both men at this discovery. But I beamed at them; and they at me. I was enjoying it. The unwonted jar beneath my feet was wrinkling my diaphragm with spasms of delight. And the fireman beamed at the engineer, with a look that said, 'See the lunatic grin; he likes it!'

"He did like it. How the iron wheels sang to me as they took the rails! How the rushing wind in my ears sang to me! From my stand on the fireman's side of the cab I could catch a glimpse of the track just ahead of the engine, where the ties seemed to leap into the throat of the mile-devouring monster. The joy of it! of seeing space swallowed by the mile!

"I shifted the eggs from hand to hand and thought of my horse, of Agassiz, of the great book, of my great luck,—luck,—luck,—until the multitudinous tongues of the thundering train were all chiming 'luck! luck! luck!' They knew! they understood! This beast of fire and tireless wheels was doing its best to get the eggs to Agassiz!

"We swung out past the Blue Hills, and yonder flashed the morning sun from the towering dome of the State House. I might have leaped from the cab and run the rest of the way on foot, had I not caught the eye of the engineer watching me narrowly. I was not in Boston yet, nor in Cambridge either. I was an escaped lunatic, who had held up a train, and forced it to carry me from Middleboro to Boston.

"Perhaps I had overdone the lunacy business. Suppose these two men should take it into their heads to turn me over to the police, whether I would or no? I could never explain the case in time to get the eggs to Agassiz. I looked at my watch. There were still a few minutes left in which I might explain to these men, who, all at once, had become my captors. But how explain? Nothing could avail against my actions, my appearance, and my little pail of sand.

"I had not thought of my appearance before. Here I was, face and clothes caked with yellow mud, my hair wild and matted, my hat gone, and in my full-grown hands a tiny tin pail of sand, as if I had been digging all night with a tiny tin shovel on the shore! And thus to appear in the decent streets of Boston of a Sunday morning!

"I began to *feel* like a lunatic. The situation was serious, or might be, and rather desperately funny at its best. I must in some way have shown my new fears, for both men watched me more sharply.

"Suddenly, as we were nearing the outer freight-yard, the train slowed down and came to a stop. I was ready to jump, but still I had no chance. They had nothing to do, apparently, but to guard me. I looked at my watch again. What time we had made! It was only six o'clock,—a whole hour left in which to get to Cambridge!

"But I didn't like this delay. Five minutes—ten—went by.

"'Gentlemen,' I began, but was cut short by an express train coming past. We were moving again, on—into a siding—on to the main track—on with a bump and a crash and a succession of crashes, running the length of the train—on, on at a turtle's pace, but on,—when the fireman, quickly jumping for the bell-rope, left the way to the step free, and—

"I never touched the step, but landed in the soft sand at the side of the track, and made a line for the freight-yard fence.

"There was no hue or cry. I glanced over my shoulder to see if they were after me. Evidently their hands were full, or they didn't know I had gone.

"But I had gone; and was ready to drop over the high board-fence, when it occurred to me that I might drop into a policeman's arms. Hanging my pail in a splint on top of a post, I peered cautiously over—a very wise thing to do before you jump a high board-fence. There, crossing the open square toward the station, was a big, burly fellow with a club—looking for me!

"I flattened for a moment, when some one in the freight-yard yelled at me. I preferred the policeman, and, grabbing my pail, I slid softly over to the street. The policeman moved on past the corner of the station out of sight. The square was free, and yonder stood a cab.

"Time was flying now. Here was the last lap. The cabman saw me coming, and squared away. I waved a dollar-bill at him, but he only stared the more. A dollar can cover a good deal, but I was too much for one dollar. I pulled out another, thrust them both at him, and dodged into the cab, calling, 'Cambridge!'

"He would have taken me straight to the police-station, had I not said, 'Harvard College. Professor Agassiz's house! I've got eggs for Agassiz,' pushing another dollar up at him through the hole.

"It was nearly half past six.

"'Let him go!' I ordered. 'Here's another dollar if you make Agassiz's house in twenty minutes. Let him out; never mind the police!'

"He evidently knew the police, or there were none around at that time on a Sunday morning. We went down the sleeping streets, as I had gone down the wood-roads from the pond two hours before, but with the rattle and crash now of a fire brigade. Whirling a corner into Cambridge Street, we took the bridge at a gallop, the driver shouting out something in Hibernian to a pair of waving arms and a belt and brass buttons.

"Across the bridge with a rattle and jolt that put the eggs in jeopardy, and on over the cobble-stones, we went. Half standing, to lessen the jar, I held the pail in one hand and held myself in the other, not daring to let go even to look at my watch.

"But I was afraid to look at the watch. I was afraid to see how near to seven o'clock it might be. The sweat was dropping down my nose, so close was I running to the limit of my time.

"Suddenly there was a lurch, and I dived forward, ramming my head into the front of the cab, coming up with a rebound that landed me across the small of my back on the seat, and sent half of my pail of eggs helter-skelter over the floor.

"We had stopped. Here was Agassiz's house; and without taking time to pick up the eggs that were scattered, I jumped out with my pail and pounded at the door.

"No one was astir in the house. But I would stir some one. And I did. Right in the midst of the racket the door opened. It was the maid.

"'Agassiz,' I gasped, 'I want Professor Agassiz, quick!' And I pushed by her into the hall.

"'Go 'way, sir. I'll call the police. Professor Agassiz is in bed. Go 'way, sir!'

"'Call him—Agassiz—instantly, or I'll call him myself.'

"But I didn't; for just then a door overhead was flung open, a great white-robed figure appeared on the dim landing above, and a quick loud voice called excitedly,—

"'Let him in! Let him in. I know him. He has my turtle eggs!'

"And the apparition, slipperless, and clad in anything but an academic gown, came sailing down the stairs.

"The maid fled. The great man, his arms extended, laid hold of me with both hands, and dragging me and my precious pail into his study, with a swift, clean stroke laid open one of the eggs, as the watch in my trembling hands ticked its way to seven—as if nothing unusual were happening to the history of the world."

CHAPTER XII
AN ACCOUNT WITH NATURE

THERE were chipmunks everywhere. The stone walls squeaked with them. At every turn, from early spring to early autumn, a chipmunk was scurrying away from me. Chipmunks were common. They did no particular harm, no particular good; they did nothing in particular, being only chipmunks and common, or so I thought, until one morning (it was June-bug time) when I stopped and watched a chipmunk that sat atop the stone wall down in the orchard. He was eating, and the shells of his meal lay in a little pile upon the big flat stone which served as his table.

They were acorn-shells, I thought; yet June seemed rather late in the season for acorns, and, looking closer, I discovered that the pile was entirely composed of June-bug shells—wings and hollow bodies of the pestiferous beetles!

Well, well! I had never seen this before, never even heard of it. Chipmunk, a *useful* member of society! actually eating bugs in this bug-ridden world of mine! This was interesting and important. Why, I had really never known Chipmunk, after all!

So I hadn't. He had always been too common. Flying squirrels were more worth while, because there were none on the farm. Now, however, I determined to cultivate the acquaintance of Chipmunk, for there might be other discoveries awaiting me. And there were.

A narrow strip of grass separated the orchard and my garden-patch. It was on my way to the garden that I most often stopped to watch this chipmunk, or rather the pair of them, in the orchard wall. June advanced, the beetles disappeared, and the two chipmunks in the wall were now seven, the young ones almost as large as their parents, and both young and old on the best of terms with me.

For the first time in four years there were prospects of good strawberries. Most of my small patch was given over to a new variety, one that I had originated; and I was waiting with an eagerness which was almost anxiety for the earliest berries.

I had put a little stick beside each of the three big berries that were reddening first (though I could have walked from the house blindfolded and picked them). I might have had the biggest of the three on June 7th, but for the sake of the flavor I thought it best to wait another day. On the 8th I went down to get it. The big berry was gone, and so was one of the others, while only half of the third was left on the vine!

Gardening has its disappointments, its seasons of despair—and wrath, too. Had a toad showed him self at that moment, he might have fared badly, for more than likely, I thought, it was he who had stolen my berries. On the garden wall sat a friendly chipmunk eying me sympathetically.

CHIPMUNK EATING JUNE-BUGS

A few days later several fine berries were ripe, and I was again on my way to the garden when I passed the chipmunks in the orchard. A shining red spot among the vine-covered stones of their wall brought me to a stop. For an instant I thought that it was my rose-breasted grosbeak, and that I was about to get a clew to its nest. Then up to the slab where he ate the June-bugs scrambled the chipmunk, and the rose-red spot on the breast of the supposed grosbeak dissolved into a big scarlet-red strawberry. And by its long wedge shape I knew it was one of my new variety.

I hurried across to the patch and found every berry gone, while a line of bloody fragments led me back to the orchard wall, where a half-dozen fresh calyx crowns completed my second discovery.

No, it did not complete it. It took a little watching to find out that the whole family—all seven!—were after those berries. They were picking them half ripe, even, and actually storing them away, canning them, down in the cavernous depths of the stone-pile!

Alarmed? Yes, and I was wrathful, too. The taste for strawberries is innate, original; you can't be human without it. But joy in chipmunks is a cultivated liking. What chance in such a circumstance has the nature-lover with the human man? What shadow of doubt as to his choice between the chipmunks and the strawberries?

I had no gun and no time to go over to my neighbor's to borrow his. So I stationed myself near by with a fistful of stones, and waited for the thieves to show themselves. I came so near to hitting one of them with a stone that the sweat started all over me. After that there was no danger. I had lost my nerve. The little scamps knew that war had been declared, and they hid and dodged and sighted me so far off that even with a gun I should have been all summer killing the seven of them.

Meantime, a good rain and the warm June days were turning the berries red by the quart. They had more than caught up to the chipmunks. I dropped my stones and picked. The chipmunks picked, too; so did the toads and the robins. Everybody picked. It was free for all. We picked them and ate them, jammed them, and canned them. I almost carried some over to my neighbor, but took peas instead.

The strawberry season closed on the Fourth of July; and our taste was not dimmed, nor our natural love for strawberries abated; but all four of the small boys had hives from over-indulgence, so bountifully did Nature provide, so many did the seven chipmunks leave us!

Peace between me and the chipmunks had been signed before the strawberry season closed, and the pact still holds. Other things have occurred since to threaten it, however. Among them, an article in a recent number of an out-of-door magazine, of wide circulation. Herein the chipmunk family was most roundly rated, in fact condemned to annihilation because of its wicked taste for birds' eggs and for the young birds. Numerous photographs accompanied the article, showing the red squirrel with eggs in his mouth, but no such proof (even the red squirrel photographs, I strongly believe, were done from a *stuffed* squirrel) of Chipmunk's guilt, though he was counted equally bad and, doubtless, will suffer with Chickaree at the hands of those who have taken the article seriously.

I believe that would be a great mistake. Indeed, I believe the article a deliberate falsehood, concocted in order to sell the made-up photographs. Chipmunk is not an egg-sucker, else I should have found it out. But of course that does not mean that no one else has found it out. It does mean, however, that if Chipmunk robs at all he does it so seldom as to call for no alarm or retribution.

There is scarcely a day in the nesting-season when I fail to see half a dozen chipmunks about the walls, yet I have never noticed one even suspiciously near a bird's nest. In an apple tree, scarcely six jumps from the home of the family in the orchard wall, a brood of tree swallows came to wing this spring; while robins, chippies, and red-eyed vireos—not tomention a cowbird, which I wish they had devoured—have also hatched and flown away from nests that these squirrels might easily have rifled.

It is not often that one comes upon even the red squirrel in the very act of robbing a nest. But the black snake, the glittering fiend! and the dear house cats! If I run across a dozen black snakes in the early summer, it is safe to say that six of them are discovered to me by the cries of the birds that they are robbing. So is it with the cats. No creature larger than a June-bug, however, is often distressed by a chipmunk. In a recent letter to me Mr. Burroughs says:—

"No, I never knew the chipmunk to suck or destroy eggs of any kind, and I have never heard of any well-authenticated instance of his doing so. The red squirrel is the sinner in this respect, and probably the gray squirrel also."

It will be difficult to find a true bill against him. Were the evidence all in, I believe that instead of a culprit we should find Chipmunk a useful citizen. Does not that pile of June-bug bodies on the flat stone leave me still in debt to him? He may err occasionally, and may, on occasion, make a nuisance of himself—but so do my four small boys, bless them! And, well,—who doesn't? When a family of chipmunks, which you have fed all summer on the veranda, take up their winter quarters inside the closed cabin, and chew up your quilts, hammocks, table-cloths, and whatever else there is of chewable properties, then they are anathema.

The havoc certain chipmunks in the mountains once made among our possessions was dreadful. But instead of exterminating them root and branch, a big box was prepared the next summer and lined with tin, in which the linen was successfully wintered.

But how real was the loss, after all? Here was a rough log cabin on the side of Thorn Mountain. What sort of table-cloth ought to be found in such a cabin, if not one that has been artistically chewed by chipmunks? Is it for fine linen that we take to the woods in summer? The chipmunks are well worth a table-cloth now and then—well worth, besides these, all the strawberries and all the oats they can steal from my small patch.

Only it isn't stealing. Since I ceased throwing stones and began to watch the chipmunks carefully, I do not find that their manner is in the least the manner of thieves. They do not act as if they were taking what they have no right to. For who has told Chipmunk to earn his oats in the sweat of his brow? No one. Instead, he seems to understand that he is one of the innumerable factors ordained to make me sweat—a good and wholesome experience for me so long as I get the necessary oats.

And I get them, in spite of the chipmunks, though I don't like to guess at the quantity of oats they have carried off—anywhere, I should say, from a peck to a bushel, which they have stored as they tried to store the berries, somewhere in the big recesses of the stone wall.

All this, however, is beside the point. It isn't a case of oats and berries against June-bugs. You don't haggle with Nature after that fashion. The farm is not a market-place where you get exactly what you pay for. You must spend on the farm all you have of time and strength and brains; but you must not expect in return merely your money's worth. Infinitely more than that, and oftentimes less. Farming is like virtue,—its own reward. It pays the man who loves it, no matter how short the crop of oats and corn.

So it is with Chipmunk. Perhaps his books don't balance—a few June-bugs short on the credit side. What then? It isn't mere bugs and berries, as I have just suggested, but stone-piles. What is the difference in value to me between a stone-pile with a chipmunk in it and one without. Just the difference, relatively speaking, between the house with my four boys in it, and the house without.

Chipmunk, with his sleek, round form, his rich color and his stripes, is the daintiest, most beautiful of all our squirrels. He is one of the friendliest of my tenants, too, friendlier even than the friendliest of my birds—Chickadee. The two are very much alike in spirit; but however tame and confiding Chickadee may become, he is still a bird and belongs to a differentand, despite his wings, lower order of beings. Chickadee is often curious about me; he can be coaxed to eat from my hand. Chipmunk is more than curious; he is interested; and it is not crumbs that he wants, but friendship. He can be coaxed to eat from my lips, sleep in my pocket, and even come to be stroked.

I have sometimes seen Chickadee in winter when he seemed to come to me out of very need for living companionship. But in the flood-tide of summer life Chipmunk will watch me from his stone-pile and tag me along with every show of friendship.

The family in the orchard wall have grown very familiar. They flatter me. One or another of them, sitting upon the high flat slab, sees me coming. He sits on the very edge of the crack, to be truthful; and if I take a single step aside toward him, he flips, and all there is left of him is a little angry squeak from the depths of the stones. If, however, I pass properly along, do not stop or make any sudden motion, he sees me past, then usually follows me, especially if I get well off and pause.

During a shower one day I halted under a large hickory just beyond his den. He came running after me, so interested that he forgot to look to his footing, and just opposite me slipped and bumped his nose hard against a stone—so hard that he sat up immediately and vigorously rubbed it. Another time he followed me across to the garden and on until he came to the barbed-wire fence along the meadow. Here he climbed a post and continued after me by way of the middle strand of the wire, wriggling, twisting, even grabbing the barbs, in his efforts to maintain his balance. He got midway between the posts, when the sagging strand tripped him and he fell with a splash into a shallow pool below. No, he did not drown, but his curiosity did get a ducking.

Did the family in the orchard wall stay together as a family for the first summer? I should like to know. As late as August they all seemed to be in the wall; for in August I cut my oats, and during this harvest we all worked together.

I mowed the oats as soon as they began to yellow, cocking them to cure for hay. It was necessary to let them "make" for six or seven days, and all this time the chipmunks raced back and forth between the cocks and the stone wall. They might have hidden their gleanings in a dozen crannies nearer at hand; but evidently they had a particular storehouse, near the home nest, where the family could get at their provisions in bad weather without coming forth.

Had I removed the stones and dug out the nest, I should have found a tunnel leading into the ground for a few feet and opening into a chamber filled with a bulky grass nest—a bed capable of holding half a dozen chipmunks—and, adjoining this, by a short passageway, the storehouse of the oats.

How many trips they made between this crib and the oat-patch, how many kernels they carried in their pouches at a trip, and how big a pile they had when all the grains were in,—these are more of the things I should like to know.

When the first frosts come, the family—if they are still a family—seek the nest in the ground beneath the stone wall. But they do not go to sleep immediately. Their outer entrances have not yet been closed. There is still plenty of fresh air and, of course, plenty of food—acorns, chestnuts, hickory-nuts, and oats. They doze quietly for a time and then they eat, pushing the empty shells and hulls into some side passage prepared beforehand to receive the débris.

But soon the frost is creeping down through the stones and earth overhead, the rains are filling the outer doorways and shutting off the supply of fresh air; and one day, though not sound sleepers, the family cuddle down and forget to wake entirely until the frost has begun to creep back toward the surface, and in through the softened soil is felt the thrill of the waking spring.

CHAPTER XIII
WOODS MEDICINE

THE real watcher in the woods usually goes off by himself. He hates to have anybody along; for Anybody wants to be moving all the time, and Anybody wants to be talking all the time, and Anybody wants to be finding a circus, or a zoo, or a natural history museum in the middle of the woods, else Anybody wishes he had stayed at home or gone to the ball-game.

Now I always say to Mr. Anybody when he asks me to take him into the woods, "Yes, come along, if you can stand stock-still for an hour, without budging; if you can keep stock-still for an hour, without talking; if you can get as excited watching two tumble-bugs trying to roll their ball up hill, as you do watching nine baseball men trying to bat their ball about a field."

The doctor pulled a small blankbook out of his vest pocket, scribbled something in Latin and Chinese (at least it looked like Chinese), and then at the bottom wrote in English, "Take one teaspoonful every hour"; and, tearing off the leaf, handed it to the patient. It was a prescription for some sort of medicine.

Now I am going to give you a prescription,—for some woods medicine,—a magic dose that will cure you of blindness and deafness and clumsy-footedness, that will cause you to see things and hear things and think things in the woods that you have never thought or heard or seen in the woods before. Here is the prescription:—

WOOD CHUCK, M. D.,

MULLEIN HILL.

Office Hours: 5.30 A.M. until Breakfast.

Rx: No moving for one hour.... No talking for one hour.... No dreaming or thumb-twiddling the while....

Sig: The dose to be taken from the top of a stump with a bit of sassafras bark or a nip of Indian turnip every time you go into the woods.

WOOD CHUCK.

I know that this compound will cure if you begin taking it early enough—along, I should say, from the Fifth to the Eighth Grades. It is a very difficult dose to take at any age, but it is almost impossible for grown-ups to swallow it; for they have so many things to do, or think they have, that they can't sit still a whole hour anywhere—a terrible waste of time! And then they have been talking for so many years that to stop for a whole hour might—kill them, who knows! And they have been working nervously with their hands so long that their thumbs will twiddle, and to sleep they will go the minute they sit down, in spite of themselves. It is no use to give this medicine to grown-ups. They are what Dr. Wood Chuck calls "chronics"—hopeless hurriers who will never sit down upon a stump, who, when the Golden Chariot comes for them, will stand up and drive all the way to heaven.

However, I am not giving this medicine to grown-ups, but to you. Of course you will make a bad face over it, too; for, young or old, it is hard to sit still and even harder to keep still—I mean not to talk. I have closely watched four small boys these several years now, and I never knew one of them to sit still for a whole hour *at home*—not once in his whole life! And as for his tongue! he might tuck that into his cheek, hold it down between his teeth, crowd it back behind his fist—no matter. The tongue is an unruly member. But let these four boys get into the woods, and every small pale-face of them turns Indian instinctively, tip-toeing up and down the ridges with lips as close-sealed as if some finger of the forest were laid upon them. So it must be with you when you enter the fields and woods.

The wood-born people are all light-footed and cautious in their stirring. Only the box turtles scuff carelessly along; and that is because they can shut themselves up—head, paws, tail—inside their lidded shells, and defy their enemies.

The skunk, however, is sometimes careless in his going; for he knows that he will neither be crowded nor jostled along the street, so he naturally behaves as if all the woods were his. Yet, how often do you come upon a skunk? Seldom—because, he is quite as unwilling to meet you as you are to meet him; but as one of your little feet makes as much noise in the leaves as all four of his, he hears you coming and turns quietly down some alley or in at some burrow and allows you to pass on.

Louder than your step in the woods is the sound of your voice. Perhaps there is no other noise so far-reaching, so alarming, so silencing in the woods as the human voice. When your tongue begins, all the other tongues cease. Songs stop as by the snap of a violin string; chatterings cease; whisperings end—mute are the woods and empty as a tomb, except the wind be moving aloft in the trees.

Three things all the animals can do supremely well: they can hear well; they can see motion well; they can wait well.

If you would know how well an animal can wait, scare Dr. Wood Chuck into his office, then sit down outside and wait for him to come out. It would be a rare and interesting thing for you to do. No one has ever done it yet, I believe! Establish a world's record for keeping still! But you should scare him in at the beginning of your summer vacation so as to be sure you have all the waiting-time the state allows: for you may have to leave the hole in September and go back to school.

When the doctor wrote the prescription for this medicine, "No moving for an hour," he was giving you a very small, a homeopathic dose of patience, as you can see; for *an hour* at a time, every wood-watcher knows, will often be only a waste of time, unless followed immediately by another hour of the same.

On the road to the village one day, I passed a fox-hunter sitting atop an old stump. It was about seven o'clock in the morning.

"Hello, Will!" I called, "been out all night?"

"No, got here 'bout an hour ago," he replied.

I drove on and, returning near noon, found Will still atop the stump.

"Had a shot yet?" I called.

"No, the dogs brought him down 'tother side the brook, and carried him over to the Shanty field."

About four o'clock that afternoon I was hurrying down to the station, and there was Will atop that same stump.

"Got him yet?" I called.

"No, dogs are fetching him over the Quarries now"—and I was out of hearing.

It was growing dark when I returned; but there was Will Hall atop the stump. I drew up in the road.

"Grown fast to that stump, Will?" I called. "Want me to try to pull you off?"

"No, not yet," he replied, jacking himself painfully to his feet. "Chillin' up some, ain't it?" he added shaking himself. "Might's well go home, I guess"—when from the direction of Young's Meadows came the eager voice of his dogs; and, waving me on, he got quickly back atop the stump, his gun ready across his knees.

I was nearly home when, through the muffle of the darkening woods, I heard the quick *bang! bang!* of Will's gun.

Yes, he got him, a fine red fox. And speaking to me about it one day, he said,—

"There's a lot more to sittin' still than most folks thinks. The trouble is, most folks in the woods can't stand the monopoly of it."

Will's English needs touching up in spots; but he can show the professors a great many things about the ways of the woods.

And now what does the doctor mean by "No dreaming or thumb-twiddling" in the woods? Just this: that not only must you be silent and motionless for hours at a time, but you must also be alert—watchful, keen, ready to take a hint, to question, guess, and interpret. The fields and woods are not full of life, but full only of the sounds, shadows, and signs of life.

You are atop of your stump, when over the ridge you hear a slow, quiet rustle in the dead leaves—a skunk; then a slow, *loud* rustle—a turtle; then a *quick*, loud—*one-two-three*—rustle—a chewink; then a tiny, rapid rustle—a mouse; then a long, rasping rustle—a snake; then a measured, galloping rustle—a squirrel; then a light-heavy, hop-thump rustle—a rabbit; then—and not once have you seen the rustlers in the leaves beyond the ridge; and not once have you stirred from your stump.

Perhaps this understanding of the leaf-sounds might be called "interpretation"; but before you can interpret them, you must hear them; and no dozing, dreaming, fuddling sitter upon a stump has ears to hear.

As you sit there, you notice a blue jay perched silent and unafraid directly over you—not an ordinary, common way for a blue jay to act. "Why?" you ask. Why, a nest, of course, somewhere near! Or, suddenly round and round the trunk of a large oak tree whirls a hummingbird. "Queer," you say. Then up she goes—and throwing your eye ahead of her through the tree-tops you chance to intercept her bee-line flight—a hint! She is probably gathering lichens for a nest which she is building somewhere near, in the direction of her flight. A whirl! a flash!—as quick as light! You have a wonderful story!

Now do not get the impression that all one needs to do in order to become acquainted with the life of the woods is to sit on a stump a long time, say nothing, and listen hard. All that is necessary—rather, the ability to do it is necessary; but in the woods or out it is also necessary to exercise common sense. Guess, for instance, when guessing is all that you can do. You will learn more, however, and learn it faster, generally, by following it up, than by sitting on a stump and guessing about it.

At twilight, in the late spring and early summer, we frequently hear a gentle, tremulous call from the woods or from below in the orchard. "What is it?" I had been asked a hundred times, and as many times had guessed that it might be the hen partridge clucking to her brood; or else I had replied that it made me think of the mate-call of a coon, or that I half inclined to believe it the cry of the woodchucks, or that possibly it might be made by the owls. In fact, I didn't know the peculiar call, and year after year I kept guessing at it.

We were seated one evening on the porch listening to the whip-poor-wills, when some one said, "There's your woodchuck singing again." Sure enough, there sounded the tremulous woodchuck-partridge-owl-coon cry. I slipped down through the birches determined at last to know that cry and stop guessing about it, if I had to follow it all night.

The moon was high and full, the footing almost noiseless, and everything so quiet that I quickly located the clucking sounds as coming from the orchard. I came out of the birches into the wood-road, and was crossing the open field to the orchard, when something dropped with a swish and a vicious clacking close upon my head. I jumped from under my hat, almost,—and saw the screech owl swoop softly up into the nearest apple tree. Instantly she turned toward me and uttered the gentle purring cluck that I had been guessing at so hard for at least three years. And even while I looked at her, I saw in the tree beyond, silhouetted against the moonlit sky, two round bunches,—young owls evidently,—which were the explanation of the calls. These two, and another young one, were found in the orchard the following day.

I rejoined the guessers on the porch and gave them the satisfying fact, but only after two or three years of guessing about it. I had laughed once at some of my friends over on the other road who had bolted their front door and had gone out of the door at the side of the house for precisely twenty-one years because the key in the front-door lock wouldn't work. They were intending to have it fixed, but the children being little kept them busy; then the children grew up, and of course kept them busier; got married at last and left home—all but one daughter. Still the locksmith was not called to fix that front door. One day this unmarried daughter, in a fit of impatience, got at that door herself, and found that the key had been inserted just twenty-one years before—*upside down!*

There I had sat on the porch—on a stump, let us say, and guessed about it. Truly, my key to this mystery had been left long in the lock, upside down, while I had been going in and out by the side door.

No, you must *go* into the fields and woods, go deep and far and frequently, with eyes and ears and all your souls alert!

NOTES AND SUGGESTIONS
CHAPTER I
TO THE TEACHER

Put the question to your scholars individually: Who is *your* messenger of spring? Make the reading of this book not an end in itself, but only a means toward getting the pupils out of doors. Never let the reading stop with the end of the chapter, any more than you would let your garden stop with the buying of the seeds. And how eager and restless a healthy child is for the fields and woods with the coming of spring! Do not let your opportunity slip. Go with them after reading this chapter (re-reading if you can the first chapter in "The Fall of the Year") out to some meadow stream where they can see the fallen stalks and brown matted growths of the autumn through which the new spring shoots are pushing, green with vigor and promise. The seal of winter has been broken; the pledge of autumn has been kept; the life of a new summer has started up from the grave of the summer past. Here by the stream under your feet is the whole cycle of the seasons—the dead stalks, the empty seed-vessels, the starting life.

Let the children watch for the returning birds and report to you; have them bring in the opening flowers, giving them credit (on the blackboard) for each *new* flower found; go with them (so that they will not *bring* the eggs to you) to see the new nests discovered, teaching them by every possible means the folly and cruelty of robbing birds' nests, of taking life; while at the same time you show them the beauty of life, its sacredness, and manifold interests.

FOR THE PUPIL

PAGE 1

Have you ever *seen* a "spring peeper" peeping? You will hear, these spring nights, many distinct notes in the marshes, and when you have seen all of the lowly musicians you will be a fairly accomplished naturalist. Let the discovery of "Who's Who among the Frogs" this spring be one of your first outdoor studies. The picture shows you Pickering's hyla, blowing his bagpipe. *Arbutus*: trailing arbutus (*Epigæa repens*), sometimes called ground-laurel, and mayflower, fishflower (in New Jersey).

hepatica: liver-leaf (*Hepatica triloba*).

Spice-bush: wild allspice, fever-bush, Benjamin-bush (*Benzoin æstivale*).

Wood-pussy: the skunk, who comes out of his winter den very early in spring, and whose scent is one of the characteristic odors of a New England spring.

PAGE 2

All white and still. The whole poem will be found on the last page of "Winter," the second book in this series.

trillium: the wake-robin. Read Mr. Burroughs's book "Wake-Robin,"—the first of his outdoor books.

PAGE 4

phœbe: See the chapter called "The Palace in the Pig-Pen."

bloodroot: *Sanguinaria canadensis*. See the picture on this page. So named because of the red-orange juice in the root-stalks, used by the Indians as a stain.

marsh-marigolds: The more common but *incorrect* name is "cowslip." The marsh-marigold is *Caltha palustris* and belongs with the buttercup and wind-flower to the Crowfoot Family. The cowslip, a species of primrose, is a European plant and belongs to the Primrose Family.

PAGE 5

woolly-bear: caterpillar of the isabella tiger moth, the common caterpillar, brown in the middle with black ends, whose hairs look as if they had been clipped, so even are they.

mourning-cloak: See picture, page 77 of "Winter," the second book of this series. The antiopa butterfly.

juncos: the common slate-colored "snowbirds."

witch-hazel: See picture, page 28 of "The Fall of the Year"; read description of it on pages 31-33 of the same volume.

bluets: or "innocence" (*Houstonia cærulea*).

PAGE 6

the Delaware: the Delaware River, up which they come in order to lay their eggs. As they come up they are caught in nets and their eggs or "roe" salted and made into caviar.

Cohansey Creek: a small river in New Jersey.

Lupton's Meadows: local name of meadows along Cohansey Creek.

CHAPTER II
TO THE TEACHER

Read Kipling's story in "The Second Jungle Book" called "The Spring Running." Both Jungle Books ought to be in your school library. Spring is felt on the ocean as well as over the land; life is all of one piece; the thrill we feel at the touch of spring is felt after his manner and degree by bird and beast and by the fish of the sea. Go back to the last paragraph of chapter I for the *thought*. Here I have expanded that thought of the tides of life rising. See the picture of the herring on their deep sea run on page 345 of the author's "Wild Life Near Home." Let the chapter suggest to the pupils the mysterious powers of the minds of the lower animals.

FOR THE PUPIL

PAGE 7

Mowgli: Do you know Mowgli of "The Jungle Book"?

Chaucer: the "Father of English Poetry." This is one of the opening lines of the Prologue to the Canterbury Tales.

PAGE 8

migrating birds: See "The Great Tidal Waves of Bird Life" by D. Lange, in the "Atlantic Monthly" for August, 1909.

PAGE 9

The cold-blooded: said of those animals lower than the mammals and birds, that have not four-chambered hearts and the complete double blood-circulation.

Weymouth Back River: of Weymouth, Massachusetts.

PAGE 10

catfish: or horn-pout or bull-pout, see picture, page 12.

PAGE 11

stickleback: The little male stickleback builds a nest, drives the female into it to lay her eggs, then takes charge of the eggs until the fry hatch out and go off for themselves.

CHAPTER III
TO THE TEACHER

You will try to get three suggestions out of this chapter for your pupils: First, that an old tree with holes may prove to be the most *fruitful* and interesting tree in the neighborhood, that is to say, nothing out of doors is so far fallen to pieces, dead, and worthless as to be passed by in our nature study. (Read to them "Second Crops" in the author's "A Watcher in the Woods.") Secondly: the humble tree-toad is well worth the most careful watching, for no one yet has told us all of his life-story. Thirdly: one of the benefits of this simple, sincere love of the out-of-doors will come to us as rest, both in mind and body, as contentment, too, and clearer understanding of what things are worth while.

FOR THE PUPIL

PAGE 14

burlap petticoat: a strip of burlap about six inches wide tied with a string and folded over about the trunks of the trees under which the night-feeding gypsy moth caterpillars hide by day. The burlaps are lifted and the worms killed.

a peddler's stall: In the days of the author's boyhood peddlers sold almost everything that the country people could want.

PAGE 16

grim-beaked baron: the little owl of the tree.

keep: an older name for castle; sometimes for the dungeon.

PAGE 20

for him to call the summer rain: alluding to his evening and his cloudy-day call as a sign of coming rain.

PAGE 22

castings: the disgorged lumps of hair and bones of the small animals eaten by the owls.

PAGE 24

Altair and Arcturus: prominent stars in the northern hemisphere.

CHAPTER IV
TO THE TEACHER

See the suggestions for the corresponding chapter in "The Fall of the Year," the first volume in this series. Lest you may not have that book at hand, let me repeat here the gist of what I said there: that you make this chapter the purpose of one or more field excursions with the class—in order to see with your own eyes the characteristic sights of spring as recorded here; secondly, that you use this, and chapters VI and X, as school tests of the pupil's knowledge and observation of his own fields and woods; and thirdly, let the items mentioned here be used as possible subjects for the pupil's further study as themes for compositions, or independent investigations out of school hours. The finest fruit the teacher can show is a school full of children personally interested in things. And what better things than live things out of doors?

CHAPTER V
TO THE TEACHER

I might have used a star, or the sun, or the sea to teach the lesson involved here, instead of the crow and his three broken feathers. But these three feathers will do for your pupils as the falling apple did for Sir Isaac Newton. The point of the chapter is: that the feathers like the stars must round out their courses; that this universe is a universe of law, of order, and of reason, even to the wing feathers of a crow. Try to show your pupils the beauty and wonder of order and law (not easy to do) as well as the beauty and wonder of shapes and colors and sounds, etc.

FOR THE PUPIL

PAGE 34

primaries, secondaries, tertials: Turn to your dictionary under "Bird" (or at the front of some good bird book) and study out just which feathers of the wing these named here are.

PAGE 35

half-moulted hen: Pick her up and notice the regular and systematic arrangement of the young feathers. Or take a plucked hen and draw roughly the pin-feather scheme as you find it on her body.

PAGE 37

reed-birds: The bobolink is also called "rice-bird" from its habit of feeding in the rice-fields of the South on its fall migration.

CHAPTER VI
FOR THE PUPIL

Do not stop doing or seeing or hearing when you have done, seen, and heard the few things suggested in this chapter and in chapters IV and X; for these are only suggestions, and merely intended to give you a start, as if your friend had said to you upon your visiting a new city, "Now, don't fail to see the Common and the old State House, etc.; and don't fail to go down to T Wharf, etc.,"—knowing that all the time you would be doing and seeing and hearing a thousand interesting things.

CHAPTER VII
TO THE TEACHER

I called this chapter when I first wrote it "The Friendship of Nature"—a much used title, but entirely suggestive of the thought and the lesson in the story here. This was first written about six years ago, and to-day, May 12, 1912, that pair of phœbes, or another pair, have their nest out under the pig-pen roof as they have had every year since I have known the pen. Repeat and expand the thought as I have put it into the mouth of Nature in the first paragraph—"We will share them [the acres] together." Instill into your pupils' minds the large meaning of obedience to Nature's laws and love for her and all her own. Show them also how ready Nature is (and all the birds and animals and flowers) to be friendly; and how even a city dooryard may hold enough live *wild* things for a small zoo. This chapter might well be made use of by the city teacher to stir her pupils to see what interesting live things their city or neighborhood has, although the woods and open fields are miles away.

FOR THE PUPIL

PAGE 48

a hornet's nest: the white-faced hornet, that builds the great cone-shaped paper nests.

swifts thunder in the chimney: See chapter VII (and notes) in "Winter." For the "thunder" see section IX in chapter X of this book.

PAGE 49

cabbage butterfly: a pest; a small whitish butterfly with a few small black spots. Its grubs eat cabbage.

PAGE 54

the crested flycatcher: is the largest of the family; builds in holes; distinguished by its use of cast-off snake-skins in its nests.

kingbird: Everybody knows him, for it is usually he who chases the marauding crows; he builds, out in the apple tree if he can, a big, bulky nest with strings a-flying from it: also called "bee-martin," a most useful bird.

wood pewee: builds on the limbs of forest trees a most beautiful nest, much like a hummingbird's, only larger. Pewee's soft, pensive call of "pe-e-e-wee" in the deep, quiet, dark-shrouded summer woods is one of the sweetest of bird notes.

chebec: a little smaller than a sparrow; builds a beautiful nest in orchard trees and says "chebec, chebec, chebec."

One had died: After phœbe brings off her first brood sprinkle a little, tobacco-dust or lice-powder, such as you use in the hen-yard, into the nest to kill the vermin. Otherwise the second and third broods may be eaten alive by lice or mites.

CHAPTER VIII
TO THE TEACHER

In "Winter" I put a chapter called "The Missing Tooth," showing the dark and bitter side of the life of the wild things; here I have taken that thought as most people think of it (see Burroughs's essay, "A Life of Fear" in "Riverby") and in the light of typical examples tried to show that wild life is not fear, but peace and joy. The kernel of the chapter is found in the words: "The level of wild life, the soul of all nature, is a great serenity." Let the pupils watch and report instances of fear (easy to see) and in the same animals instances of peace and joy.

FOR THE PUPIL

PAGE 60

gray harrier: so named because of his habit of flying low and "harrying," that is, hunting, catching small prey on or near the ground. "Harry" comes from the Anglo-Saxon word for army.

PAGE 61

"He looketh as it were a grym leoun": from Chaucer's description of the Cock in the story of the Cock and the Fox.

PAGE 62

terrible pike: closely related to the pickerel.

kingfisher: builds in holes in sand-banks near water. Its peculiar rattle sounds like the small boys' "clapper."

PAGE 63

"The present only toucheth thee?": Burns's poem "To a Mouse."

PAGE 64

"The fair music that all creatures made": from Milton's poem "To a Solemn Music," "solemn" meaning "orchestral" music.

PAGE 65

then doubling once more: This is all figurative language. I am thinking of myself as the fox. The dogs have run themselves to death on my trail, and I am turning back, "doubling," to have a look at them and to rejoice over their defeat.

PAGE 71

pine marten: The marten is so rare in this neighborhood that I am inclined to think the creature was the large weasel.

PAGE 73

the heavy bar across their foreheads: a very unusual way of yoking oxen in the United States. The only team I ever saw here so yoked.

PAGE 74

San Francisco: alluding to the earthquake and fire which nearly wiped out the city in 1906.

CHAPTER IX
FOR THE PUPIL

The picture of the young buzzard is as true as a photograph; the bumped-up drawing of the old bird looks precisely as she did atop her dead tree, watching my approach. This vulture rarely soars into New England skies; down South, especially along the coast, the smaller black vulture (*Catharista urubu*) is found very tame and in great abundance; while in the far Southwest lives the great condor.

PAGE 80

tulip poplar: tulip-tree (*Liriodendron tulipifera*).

"For it had bene an auncient tree": from Edmund Spenser's "Shepherd's Calendar."

PAGE 85

a dozen kinds of cramps: Perhaps you will say I didn't find much in finding the buzzard's nest, and got mostly cramps! Yes, but I also got the buzzard's nest—a thing that I had wanted to see for many years. It was worth seeing, however, for its own sake. Even a buzzard is interesting. See the account of him in "Wild Life Near Home," the chapter called "A Buzzard's Banquet."

CHAPTER XI
TO THE TEACHER

The point of the story is the enthusiasm of the naturalists for their work—work that to the uncaring and unknowing seemed not even worth while. But all who do great things do them with all their might. No one can stop to count the cost whose soul is bent on great things.

FOR THE PUPIL

PAGE 94

Burlington: in Vermont.

Concord and Middleboro: in Massachusetts.

Zadoc Thompson: a Vermont naturalist.

D. Henry Thoreau: better known as Henry D. Thoreau; author of "Walden," etc.

J. W. P. Jenks: for many years head of Pierce Academy, Middleboro, and later Professor of Agricultural Zoölogy in Brown University.

PAGE 96

Contributions: used in place of the whole name: Go yourself into the public library and read this and look at the four large volumes.

PAGE 101

spatter-docks: yellow pond-lily (*Nuphar advena*).

PAGE 102

dinosaurian: one of the fossil reptile monsters of the Mesozoic, or "middle," period of the earth's history, before the age of man.

CHAPTER XII
TO THE TEACHER

In this story I have tried to settle the difficult question of debit and credit between me and the out-of-doors. Shall we exterminate the red squirrels, the hawks, owls, etc., is a question that is not so easily answered as one might think. The fact is we do not want to exterminate *any* of our native forms of life—we need them all, and owe them more, each of them, for the good they do us, than they owe us for the little harm they may do us. Read this over with the children with its moral and economic lesson in view. Send to the National Association of Audubon Societies, New York City, for their free leaflets upon this matter. The Pennsylvania Department of Agriculture, Harrisburg, Pa., has a bulletin upon this same subject which will be sent free upon application.

FOR THE PUPIL

PAGE 115

June-bug: the very common brown beetle whose big white grubs you dig up under the sod and in composts.

PAGE 118

rose-breasted grosbeak: one of the most beautiful of our birds, and a lovely singer.

PAGE 120

Chickaree: the common name of the red squirrel. The red squirrel does not need to be destroyed.

tree swallows: They build in holes in orchard trees, etc.; to be distinguished on the wing from the barn swallows by their white bellies and plain, only slightly forked tails.

chippies: the little chipping sparrow, or hair-bird.

red-eyed vireos: the most common of the vireos; see picture of its nest on page 40 of "Winter."

PAGE 121

cowbird: the miserable brown-headed blackbird that lays its egg or eggs in smaller birds' nests and leaves its young to be fed by the unsuspecting foster-mother. As the young cowbird is larger than the rightful young, it gets all the food and causes them to starve.

PAGE 122

Thorn Mountain: one of the smaller of the White Mountains; it overlooks the village of Jackson, N. H.

CHAPTER XIII
TO THE TEACHER

If you have read through "The Fall of the Year" and "Winter" and to this chapter in "The Spring of the Year," you will know that the upshot of these thrice thirteen readings has been to take you and your children into the woods; you will know that the last paragraph of this last chapter is the aim and purpose and key of all three books. You must *go* into the woods, you must lead your children to go, deep and far and frequently. The Three R's first—but after them, before dancing, or cooking, or sewing, or manual training, or anything, send your children out into the open, where they belong. The school can give them nothing better than the Three R's, and can only fail in trying to give them more, except it give them the freedom of the fields. Help Nature, the old nurse, to take your children on her knee.

FOR THE PUPIL

PAGE 128

Here is the prescription: Think you can swallow it? Go out and try.

PAGE 129

Golden Chariot: In what Bible story does the Golden Chariot descend? and whom does it carry away?

pale-face: an Indian name for the white man.

PAGE 130

box turtles: They are sometimes found as far north as the woods of Cape Cod, Massachusetts; but are very abundant farther south.

PAGE 133

Chewink: towhee, or ground-robin; to be distinguished by his loud call of "chewink" and his vigorous scratching among the leaves.

Made in the USA
Middletown, DE
14 February 2025

71371953R00024